DEDICATED NURSE

DEDICATED NURSE

Valerie Scott

1026353

Chivers Press • G.K. Hall & Co.
Bath, England • Thorndike, Maine USA

This Large Print edition is published by Chivers Press, England, and by G.K. Hall & Co., USA.

Published in 2000 in the U.K. by arrangement with Robert Hale Ltd.

Published in 2000 in the U.S. by arrangement with Robert Hale Ltd.

U.K. Hardcover ISBN 0-7540-3935-8 (Chivers Large Print)
U.K. Softcover   ISBN 0-7540-3936-6 (Camden Large Print)
U.S. Softcover   ISBN 0-7838-8761-2 (Nightingale Series Edition)

The text of this Large Print edition is unabridged.
Other aspects of the book may vary from the original edition.

Set in 16 pt. New Times Roman.

Printed in Great Britain on acid-free paper.

British Library Cataloguing in Publication Data available

Library of Congress Cataloging-in-Publication Data

Scott, Valerie, 1928–
       Dedicated nurse / by Valerie Scott.
             p.   cm.
       ISBN 0-7838-8761-2 (lg. print : sc : alk. paper)
       1. Large type books.   I. Title.
       [PR6069.C615D44   2000]
       823'.914—dc21   99–41969

DEDICATED NURSE

CHAPTER ONE

Andrea Chaston stepped off the bus at the hospital gates and paused to brush a strand of her long chestnut hair from her pale green eyes. The sunlight of early summer seemed too strong for her already at this hour, and she was beginning to dread the long hours ahead, when she would be facing Simon Morrell across the operating table in Theatre. She caught her breath in a little sigh as she thought of Simon, and she passed between the opened gates and walked swiftly towards the main entrance to the hospital, her long legs carrying her tall, slender figure on the same route she had been following almost daily for the past three years.

But each day seemed to find a little more reluctance in her approach. She had been aware of it with rising concern for quite some time. It wasn't that she disliked the job as Theatre Sister! This was her whole life! She was one of those dedicated nurses who didn't care about the long hours and the harsh routines. Yet there was a limit to what she could take in the situation that had developed in the department, and she knew she was losing her stamina to resist the growing impulses to rebel. There were two reasons for her attitude—Simon Morrell himself, and her immediate superior Sister Cole!

1

'Sister Chaston!' The male voice reached through her thoughts and brought Andrea back to stark reality. She turned swiftly, in mid-stride, and her pale eyes seemed to glint like a black panther's in the harsh sunlight as she saw Simon Morrell hurrying towards her from the nearby car park. 'Just a word in your ear, Sister,' he said curtly as he reached her side. 'We've got a major operation later this afternoon, and I'm wondering what we can do about arrangements beforehand. There's that short list of Ops this morning, and then you're standing by on Emergency, aren't you?'

'No, Mr Morrell, this is my afternoon off!'

'Oh!' He thrust out his underlip as he stared impersonally at her, his brown eyes gleaming in the early morning brightness, and the roar of the passing London suburb traffic added an ominous background of tension to his curt tones. 'This is a damned nuisance!'

'I'll come in to work with you if you wish!' Andrea stared into his face, filled with an intense longing which she immediately tried to suppress. In the three months that he'd been at St Catherine's, Andrea had fallen in love with him, and it was this fact, coupled with the petty jealousies in the department and the overbearing manner of Sister Cole, the Theatre Superintendent, that caused Andrea so much heart-searching and torment. But he didn't know that she was human beneath her starched uniform. He hadn't paid her the smallest compliment, except where her duties were concerned, and rumour had it that he was not flesh and blood himself but some kind of robot whose sole ambition was to be the perfect surgeon.

Simon's reputation had preceded him, and the past three months had borne out that reputation. But he was hard on Andrea, who acted as a buffer between him and the rest of their surgical team, although he never expected more than was humanly possible.

'I wish the rest of the female staff were like you, Sister!' His voice was harsh although he was paying her a compliment, and she imagined he was only trying to smooth the way for his request that she forget about her half day.

'We all do what we must,' she replied, her face expressionless. 'But if you consult Sister Cole about this she'll arrange for me to take another afternoon off.'

They continued walking towards the entrance to the hospital, and Andrea found herself wishing that they were off duty together somewhere out of town, alone and happy in their own sweet company. Her imagination was so strong that a pang stabbed through her breast at the thought of so much happiness such an outing would give to her, and she stole a glance at his handsome profile. He was the cause of much speculation among the nurses at the hospital, and had been from the very moment he arrived. But he'd quickly proved that he had no time for anything outside his own small, personal sphere of activities. Women just did not figure in his calculations, and it seemed that in his professional eyes, nurses were the lowest form of life.

'Hello there,' a voice hailed them, and Andrea paused as David Hewitt, their Anaesthetist, came up.

'Good morning, David!' Simon said curtly, and he continued through the doorway, pausing only to glance at Andrea. 'I'll have a word with Sister Cole now. You are prepared to come in this afternoon?'

'Certainly!' Andrea nodded, and she found that she was holding her breath as he nodded and turned away to disappear within the great building.

'Well!' David smiled, his blue eyes glinting as he looked fondly into Andrea's lovely but sombre face. He was a jolly man, unflappable in the direst emergency, a steady influence in the seemingly endless emotional upheavals that attended them in their daily routines. 'That man doesn't know the meaning of rest, does he? I don't think he's taken a day off since he came here! And now he's got you coming in on your free time! I was waiting for it to happen. You should put your foot down, Andrea.'

'You'll be in yourself this afternoon for the

4

big Op,' she said, smiling as they continued into the hospital and made their way to the Theatre block.

'Of course! I'm always here like the rest of you!' He sighed heavily, and already there were tiny beads of sweat on his smooth, fleshy face. 'It's going to be damned hot again in Theatre today. When are they going to do something about the defect in the ventilation system?'

'They won't make any structural alterations while there's still talk of building that complete new Surgical Block!' Andrea felt her steps lagging a little at the thought of seeing Sister Cole as they went along the tiled corridor that led to their department. There was such bitter-sweet experience here! If it were not for Sister Cole, and if Simon Morrell gave even the slightest sign that he was aware of her, Andrea would be perfectly happy. But Sister Cole seemed to get worse instead of better, and Simon was so set in his ways that nothing short of an earthquake would change him.

'I think all this talk of the new wing is the cause of the trouble we're getting,' David said grimly. 'Everyone is looking for promotion.' He smiled gravely as their eyes met. At forty-five, he was like a father to her. Andrea, who was twenty-nine, had always looked upon him as a father figure, and that was the kind of interest he took in her. Three years together in the same surgical team had brought them close together, and Andrea could address him by his first name and regard herself as his equal, which was something which wouldn't happen in a hundred years with Simon Morrell.

'Except you and I, David,' she said quietly. Her pale green eyes seemed to gleam as they paused in the corridor outside the office she shared with Sister Cole.

'We're different,' he agreed, nodding. 'But even Clifford is beginning to look for his creeping shoes. Have you noticed him around Sir Humphrey lately?'

'I notice him all the time. I have to!' A grim note sounded in Andrea's gentle voice. 'He's chasing me with more fervour than ever.'

'I'd chase you myself if I were twenty years younger!' David retorted roguishly.

Andrea smiled as she opened the door of the office, and David grinned at her and placed a friendly hand upon her shoulder as he went on his way. She knew her life would be a whole lot worse if David were not around. He was such a nice person, and she could never understand why his wife had left him! He had the kind of temperament she was already wishing Simon possessed.

Simon was in the office, standing in front of Sister Cole's desk, and Andrea caught her breath as she looked into the rather plain, tense face of her immediate superior. Sister Cole looked up from her staff-duties sheet and flashed a scowl at Andrea, then dropped her gaze to her watch. But Andrea knew she was not late, and she moved to her own smaller desk in the far left corner of the office. She was aware that Simon studied her as she sat down, and then she realized that she hadn't spoken to Sister Cole.

'Good morning, Sister!' she said in gentle tones that did not betray the slightest tremor.

'Good morning,' came the sharp response. 'You're agreeable to coming in on duty this afternoon, are you?' Iris Cole, at thirty-eight, looked at least five years older, and responsibility didn't appear to sit well upon her thin shoulders. She was of medium height, with intense brown eyes deepset in wrinkled sockets. She was another who didn't care about romance, and as far as Andrea knew, there had never been a man in her superior's Spartan life.

'I'll come in if I'm needed! I've got nothing special to do.' Andrea glanced at Simon and saw that he was regarding her intently. She caught her breath as a host of powerful emotions flared up inside her, and she had to fight down the tingling sensation that threatened to overwhelm the barriers she had put up against him.

'Well that's all right then! Make your own arrangements with Sister Chaston, Mr Morrell!' Sister Cole was always meticulously correct with the surgeons. She worked with Sir Humphrey, the senior surgeon, using the best of the equipment and the largest of the four Theatres in the department. 'Sister, I'll mark you down for having Friday afternoon off instead of this afternoon. I'll take Thursday afternoon instead now. It will mean working out a new set of standby duties, but I'll attend to that when I've got the morning behind me. I'm due in Theatre now!'

'We're about ready to start ourselves,' Simon said with asperity, and he glanced at Andrea as he turned to the door. 'The first patient will be on the table in Theatre at exactly nine-fifteen, Sister!'

'We'll be ready,' Andrea said formally. She was thinking that these two were of a kind in some respects, and although she did not dislike Sister Cole—she had too much respect for her superior's skill—she could not help wondering what it was that affected both these clever people in much the same way.

'I want to talk to you, Sister!' Iris Cole looked at Andrea as the door closed behind Simon. Andrea was listening to the fading sound of his receding footsteps, and she made an effort to force her attention to remain upon her superior's words. 'What's the trouble in your Theatre? I've been getting complaints from the nurses. You are in charge of the nursing staff under you, and it's up to you to see that everything goes off smoothly.'

'I don't suppose I need to ask who's been complaining,' Andrea retorted, not liking the

8

sharpness in Sister Cole's voice. She was thinking how strange it was that they had never been on first-name terms. But it was not surprising for Sister Cole lived remotely in her own vinegary little world. 'Nurse Harmer again! She does not pay enough attention to her work. Mr Morrell is quite right to chase her when she fails in her duties. Because she is such a friend of yours I can't do anything with her!' Andrea stared straight into her superior's dark gaze.

'You should do something about the situation!' Sister Cole's lips were pinched into an uncompromising line. She was breathing heavily, a habit of hers these days when she was impatient or aroused, which seemed to be all the time.

'I've tried to take Nurse Harmer in hand, but there's a streak of wilfulness in her that I can't overcome. She's certain that she knows it all. I think she's jealous of me because I'm only two years her senior but I've made much more progress.'

'So that's what you think!' There was no indication now of Sister Cole's manner as she spoke.

'That's it exactly!' Andrea knew Nurse Harmer was a very close friend of her superior's, and she had long wondered what the two had in common. They invariably went out together when their off-duty periods coincided, and they certainly had similar temperaments. Nurse Harmer, Andrea had always found, was a sullen type, dark and rather plain, and with no interest in men. In point of fact she was exactly the kind of person Andrea had suspected Sister Cole of being at Nurse Harmer's age. There had to be some truth in that old saying about birds of a feather!

'Perhaps you are a little too young for this position you hold! A Sister in charge of a Theatre has to be in command of the entire proceedings. It's all right knowing all the latest techniques!' The faintest trace of a sneer sounded momentarily and Andrea stifled a sigh. 'But there are other things to be considered. In the old days a nurse didn't gain promotion until she had really proved herself!'

'I'm not under discussion here, Sister,' Andrea reminded gently. 'We don't have to go into my record.'

The silence that followed was tense and overpowering, and Sister Cole's dark eyes glittered savagely. Andrea felt the closeness of the room begin to stifle her, and she realized that this confrontation over the staff might lead to the very climax she had been hoping to avoid. Her instincts warned her subconsciously. Sister Cole had been looking for trouble for a long time. But it was not in Andrea's gentle nature to argue or show anger. The very fact that she was beginning to stand up to her superior proved just how badly this war of nerves was affecting her.

'I'm very well aware of what is under discussion here, Sister. But Nurse Harmer is in your team and it's up to you to help her along. I want you to do what you can to help her. I suppose you've forgotten the times you were helped as a nurse.'

'As she is such a close friend of yours it might be a better idea if she joined your team,' Andrea said pointedly.

'I've noticed recently a tendency in you to try and usurp my authority in this department!' The accusation came out of the blue and made Andrea gasp.

'What on earth do you mean, Sister?' Andrea could feel colour flaming into her cheeks, and she took a deep breath as she tried to control her fluttering emotions. 'If there is anything wrong in this department then it is up to you to put matters right.'

'So you do have something on your mind!' Sister Cole's eyes glinted.

Andrea glanced at her watch and shook her head slowly. 'I have to be getting into Theatre,' she said tremulously. 'Perhaps we'd better pursue this matter later.'

'We certainly will!' There was a note of ominous determination in Sister Cole's heavy tones. 'I'm not satisfied with the way you carry out your duties, Sister!'

'Very well!' Andrea tightened her lips on an angrier retort which rose unbidden to her lips, and she moved to the door of the office, trembling with indignation and frightened of the power of her feelings.

But there was no need for all this anger, she thought as she went along to her Theatre. Everyone had to concentrate completely upon the duties to be performed, and personal worries had no place in a nurse's mind when a patient lay upon the operating table awaiting surgery.

She found her two nurses in Theatre, busy there with last minute preparations. Nurse Whittaker was tall, a slim redhead who was ideal for Theatre. She smiled a greeting at Andrea, who nodded and smiled briefly in acknowledgement. But it was Nurse Harmer who occupied Andrea's attention. She received a brief nod and a surly glance from the girl, and Andrea went to meet her, determined to take the initiative from the outset. There was only one way to handle a situation like this.

'Nurse Harmer, I want to talk to you for a moment.'

'I'm behind with my work, Sister,' came the sulky reply, and the girl glanced at the clock on the wall. 'The first patient will be in before I'm finished if I'm not careful.'

'You're not careful enough by far,' Andrea said firmly, 'and you make matters worse by telling tales to Sister Cole. I've just been talking about you. I think you've been a nurse

12

long enough to understand that friendship counts for little in a place like this. You're part of our team, and if you can't pull your weight then you will have to go, and nothing Sister Cole can do will help you.'

'Did Sister Cole agree with you?' There seemed to be a cheeky expression in the girl's dark eyes, and Andrea felt that the veins of awkwardness in this girl and Sister Cole were similar. She could not help wondering if it was the effect one had upon the other.

'I doubt if Sister Cole will want you to go, but I'd like to know why you are not working in her team, seeing that you're both so friendly. Sister Cole takes only the very best in this department, and if your work was of any standard at all she would have had you in her team instead of pushing you on to me.'

'Are you going to victimize me because Sister Cole is on my side?' Nurse Harmer demanded.

'You know better than that, but you'd better not make any mistakes today,' Andrea warned. 'Mr Morrell gets a mean look in his eye now when your name is mentioned. If he gets any more trouble from you then all the Sister Coles in the world won't save you. But get on with your work and let's have you ready when it's time for the first patient to be brought in.'

Andrea turned away before the girl could make any comment. She went into the anteroom to scrub up at one of the sinks, and

David Hewitt appeared in the doorway at her back. Andrea dipped her hands into a bowl of antiseptic, frowning a little, her lovely face set in harsh lines. There were nagging thoughts in the back of her mind which she did not like.

'Don't look so worried,' David said slowly. 'It may never happen, you know.'

'You startled me!' Andrea glanced at him, smiling ruefully. 'Are you ready for Theatre?'

'Not quite. I'm on my way to the patient as soon as I've checked my equipment. But you're looking a bit flustered. Not more trouble, is there?'

'Nothing more than usual,' she retorted, suppressing a sigh. 'I don't know why people can't live in perpetual harmony, do you, David?'

'I wish I knew the answer to that one,' he said slowly, shaking his head. His blue eyes were serious for once. Then he smiled as he met her gaze. 'If they were all like you there would be perfect harmony! But I can't help wondering what induced Sister Cole to become a nurse in the first place. She hasn't got the right temperament for the job! She would be more suited to the job of wardress in a prison! One expects a nurse to be like you, Andrea!'

'Thank you!' She spoke lightly, hurrying a little now in order to have sufficient time to carry out her routine checks. 'You always say the right things, David.'

14

'I'm old enough to know the right thing at the right time,' he retorted, and moved away, smiling cheerfully.

Andrea was soon gowned and gloved, and a glance at the clock on the wall sent a shiver through her. She had never been late before, but today looked like being the first time. Anyone but Simon Morrell might overlook a slight delay, but she knew it would be the last straw for her overwrought nerves if he came into Theatre and reprimanded her.

She hurriedly checked her trolleys, following a routine which had become second nature to her. The instruments were laid up: clamps, forceps, retractors, and sutures were folded carefully in a sterile towel; heavy silk and fine linen thread, the first for stay sutures and the others for ligatures. She had hardly managed to check upon the work of the nurses before Nurse Whittaker was at her side, informing her that the first patient was down from the ward.

'They've started the drip, Sister,' the girl reported. 'The path-lab have sent the blood over and I've put it in the fridge.'

Andrea suppressed a sigh as she nodded, and now her personal thoughts were slipping away, leaving her mind free and clear for the job in hand. She saw the theatre orderly appear and latch back the doors of the anaesthetics room, and her heart seemed to miss a beat when Simon Morrell appeared

15

from scrubbing up, accompanied by the RSO. They were deep in conversation, no doubt discussing the case in hand, and a third figure joined them, to pause at their side before coming across to where Andrea stood. It was Clifford Stevens, a junior surgeon who would be assisting, and he let his eyes show that he was smiling behind his mask.

'Hello, Andrea, what about this evening? May I take you out?'

She shook her head automatically, almost not hearing his words. He never failed to ask that question whenever they met, and she always refused. There were a lot of rumours around the hospital about his chances with her, and she didn't doubt that he had spread most of them himself, but she knew without doubt that he was wasting his time.

Andrea glanced at him, checking that he was correctly attired. That was a part of her job, and she let her pale eyes take in the tall figure of Simon, then the shorter RSO. They were in caps, gowns, masks and white Wellingtons.

The patient was wheeled in, and Andrea knew there would be no time to carry out further checks. David Hewitt was with the patient, at the head of the trolley, guiding the anaesthetics machine and watching the vital tubing connecting it to the patient. A nurse was on one side, holding the intravenous flask. The patient was transferred to the operating table, and tension seemed to close in around Andrea more tightly than she could ever remember.

She moved her trolleys into position near the table as the stretcher trolley was wheeled out, and then the swing doors were closed. Heat seemed to build up in the theatre almost at once, and Andrea tried to drag her thoughts away from the summery day outside. It was difficult to believe that the sun was shining brightly outside this sterile surgical world of theirs. As Simon moved towards the patient she had the strange but wistful hope that one day she might be out walking with him, happy and carefree in his wonderful company.

'Sister!' Simon's harsh voice cut across her thoughts, and her mind almost went blank. She met his dark gaze. Only his bright brown eyes showed above his mask, but she could guess at the tight expression on his face. He never seemed to relax, and she couldn't remember seeing him really happy. 'Are we quite ready?' he demanded in a tone which suggested that he realized she had been day-dreaming.

She flushed, and was glad the surgical mask covered most of her face. Glancing around, she took in the positions of her nurses, gave one of her trolleys a little push, and then met his gaze, having to struggle to keep her eyes expressionless.

'We're quite ready, Mr Morrell,' she retorted, and there was just the faintest trace of a tremor in her musical voice. If only he could show that he was human, she thought remotely. If he would break down just once to let her know that he was not just a surgical machine. But there seemed little hope of that, and her unrequited love ran like a fever through her veins. She poised herself for the commencement of the operation, tense and despairing for the future, and she realized that this dangerous state of affairs could not go on. If Fate did not come to her aid then she would have to take the steps herself that were necessary to break this deadlock!

CHAPTER TWO

Simon glanced at the clock on the theatre wall before returning his gaze to Andrea's steady eyes. Now she had a preparation mop in one gloved hand, holding it out ready for use. He nodded slightly then sent a sharp glance to the head of the table, where David Hewitt was seated on his stool, adjusting his machine and ensuring that everything was within his reach.

'All right, David?' There was no impatience in Simon's tones, and he seemed steady and completely relaxed as he awaited the word to begin.

'He's all yours.' Hewitt glanced at Andrea, and she saw his right eye close in a wink.

Simon took the ready mop from Andrea's hand, and her breath stopped in her throat for a moment, threatening to stifle her. But she forced away the overpowering sense of suffocation and immediately prepared another mop, dipping it into the pot of antiseptic skin paint, watching Simon's gloved hands as he painted the area of skin exposed on the patient where he would operate. He took the second mop, and now Andrea's mind was completely free of her personal thoughts.

She took up the first sterile towel and handed it to the waiting RSO. Then she handed the towel clips to Simon, and relief was beginning to steal through her as the routine started. This was a skilled team, and they had worked together many times.

The operation began and Andrea, as always, watched Simon's delicate movements as he worked. His hands were swift and sure, as if possessed of individual awareness, and the heavy silence was broken from time to time by his curt voice as he gave instructions to his assistants.

'More fine mops, Sister,' he suddenly rapped, and he paused momentarily to glance at her as he reached out for the first of them.

She could not tell if he smiled, but his eyes had a strange intensity in their dark depths, and Andrea took a long, silent breath as they went on.

'Large clamps . . . rib retractor . . .

19

suction ... stay sutures ... large mops!' The orders came steadily, without hesitation.

Andrea cast a quick glance at the clock. Time always seemed to stand still when an operation was in progress. Time was unnecessary here. Simon had a kind of clock in his brain which told him all he needed at any stage of the operation. He was governed only by his needs and his actions were economical, studied, and very skilled.

'Fine stitch, Sister!'

Andrea was startled, shocked that her mind had started wandering slightly. She had pride in being able to anticipate the surgeon's slightest requirement, and usually she had the necessary instrument in her gloved hand, waiting for him to take it when needed. He couldn't be made to wait! He relied upon her, his skill dependent upon hers for smoothness and accurate speed.

But outside her small circle of concentration she was aware of movement in the background, and the sounds that had become so much a part of her daily life. The theatre orderly was busy doing his work and the nurses were moving ceaselessly as they followed their routine. A junior nurse approached and topped up Andrea's lotion bowl with hot saline. Then Nurse Harmer dropped something heavy on the far side of the theatre, and for a moment everything stopped and something seemed to strike

20

Andrea right through the heart. Simon looked around quickly, then turned back to stare at Andrea as if it had been her fault. She stifled a sigh behind her clammy face mask and they all tried to repair their shattered concentration.

They were approaching the climax of the operation, and tension seemed to be building up, layer upon layer until it seemed that they would all be stifled. Andrea felt herself sway once or twice, and she wriggled her toes in her boots as she tried to maintain her skilled poise.

Simon was now stitching deep inside the incision he had made, and his assistants were poised around him, all concentrating upon the motionless figure upon the table, whose life depended absolutely on their skill and judgement. The RSO and Clifford Stevens were holding clamps to steady the work, each knowing that the slightest movement would hinder Simon, who was now working as swiftly as possible, fighting against time, against the remorseless sweep of the large red second-hand on the clock. He was also fighting an inner battle against the temptation to hurry because there was barely time, and yet time had to be made.

The theatre orderly approached Andrea and waited silently for her to glance at him. When she did he made a quick motion, as if lifting a cup to his lips and drinking. Andrea glanced quickly at the clock, then sought his gaze again, and nodded. He went off for his elevenses, and when he returned the nurses would each take a turn to go.

Suddenly Simon straightened and shrugged his shoulders, and they all seemed to relax, although the tensest moment of all was approaching. Andrea found herself breathing a silent prayer as the first clamp was released. She was guarding the stay sutures, and she handed a sucker to Simon, who was peering into the depths of the cavity.

She saw the second clamp come away, and her breath seemed to stick in her throat. Tension grew again, and although the heat was almost intolerable Andrea felt like ice inside. She saw sweat beading Simon's forehead, and longed to reach out and wipe it away, but her concentration was upon her work. Then the stay sutures were released, and she had a stitch ready, her gaze fixed upon Simon. He looked up at her suddenly, almost surprising her, and he shook his head.

'It's all right, I shan't need that, Sister!'

At his words the tension seemed to flee. He meant that the suture line was holding. The operation itself was a success, barring complications. Andrea felt herself float down slowly from the high pinnacles of alertness and tension, and she discovered that her body was sticky with the heat and that she ached in every muscle from cramp because of her crouched position over her trolleys. She realized that the operation had lasted two and a half hours.

The atmosphere in the theatre was steamy, and Andrea's mask was sticking to her face. But there was still much to be done and they could not afford to relax. She saw the orderly return, and she was ready with a nod when she caught Nurse Whittaker's eye. The nurse departed for her break.

But the end of the operation was in sight, and Andrea signalled for Nurse Harmer to check the mops. Everything had to be accounted for before the surgeon could begin to close the incision.

'I'm ready for closing, Sister,' Simon said almost immediately, and now there was the faintest trace of weariness in his tones.

Andrea glanced quickly along the rows of mops, and checked her total against the numbers chalked up on the blackboard.

'All mops accounted for,' she retorted thankfully.

Simon nodded, then glanced at the anaesthetist. 'How is he doing at your end, David?'

'Fine,' Hewitt replied.

'Good!' Simon straightened once more and glanced around, his mask taut over his nose and mouth as he took a deep breath. He looked at the RSO. 'Would you do the skin sutures? I want to get my report done as quickly as possible.'

He stepped away from the table, and Andrea's pale eyes followed his movement.

The RSO assumed Simon's place, but before he could continue the work, Simon paused by the swing doors, his mask untied and dangling upon his chest. There was a thin smile upon his damp face as he called to them.

'Thank you, everyone. It was a fine job.'

The nurses began bustling around, already beginning to clean up in readiness for the next case, and Andrea signalled to the orderly, who departed to deliver a message to the maid to prepare coffee and then to collect the bed for the patient. The anaesthetics machine was switched off, and moments later the patient was removed by a ward nurse and the orderly. Andrea gave the ward nurse details of the operation, and sighed heavily as she removed her face mask. Nurse Whittaker helped her out of her heavy gown, and it was like escaping from prison.

But Andrea, finding time now for a few personal thoughts, had the strange feeling that she would never escape the prison her life had become. Sister Cole was her jailer here at the hospital, harsh and unrelenting. There was no determinate sentence! Each succeeding day was like all those preceding ones where tension, drama and human conflicts erupted continuously to make their demanding duties all the more difficult. Yet one clear fact seemed to stare Andrea boldly in the face. All this trouble was becoming too much for her nerves and her peace of mind. And she had the feeling that the situation could only become worse!

The work of cleaning up after the operation continued, and Andrea put the instruments from her tray into the lotion bowl. The theatre was in some disorder, and Nurse Harmer was skulking in the background, her face showing its habitual scowl now her mask was removed. The girl looked a lot older than twenty-six, Andrea thought as she went around the theatre, fighting off her fatigue. David Hewitt was making an entry in the Dangerous Drugs book.

'That's a good one to have behind us,' he remarked as Andrea passed him. He closed the book, his blue eyes serious as he looked at her. 'I'm not looking forward to this afternoon, are you?'

'Not in the least!' Andrea shook her head slowly. 'I don't know, David, but I have the uncanny feeling that everything is rapidly becoming all too much for me.'

'Not sickening for something, are you?' He subjected her to such a concerned stare that she had to smile.

'I don't think so! It's all in my mind really! I think it's because Sister Cole wants me to feel this way. I'm sure that's why she treats me as she does. She knows it will gradually wear me down and make my work suffer.'

'Well I can see matters coming to a head before very long.' David was serious, which was most unusual for him. 'I'd like to know what's got into Iris Cole. She was never of a really pleasant nature, God knows! But she's getting worse day by day. I don't know how you managed to put up with her this long, Andrea. But our work is getting more complicated all the time, and one needs a clear mind in an operation. Sister Cole ought to know better! I've a good mind to talk to her myself.'

'Please don't, David!' Alarm showed in Andrea's pale green eyes as she stared at his intent face. 'I'm sure it would only make matters worse. I know it would. I shall just have to wait it out and hope to discover what it is that's niggling Sister Cole.' A sad smile touched her lips. 'I suppose I could always look for a similar position in another hospital if this one gets too much for me.'

'Nonsense!' He shook his head immediately. 'That's out of the question. We would miss you more than we'd miss Sister Cole herself, although she is your superior. She's just a jealous woman who is realizing that age is beginning to catch up on her.'

'But she's only thirty-eight!'

'And she knows she's about ten years older than you, and that you're a better theatre Sister now than she could ever hope to be. I'm serious about this, Andrea! I've been watching you this morning, and it was easy to see that this situation is beginning to affect you. I'm not going to stand by and watch your life go to pieces because of some obscure emotion troubling Sister Cole. I'm going to try and draw her out a little and find what is weighing so heavily upon her mind. There must be something because she isn't performing her duties to the best of her ability. It is noticeable that she is labouring under some burden.'

'I don't know, I'm sure!' Andrea turned away with a sigh. 'But it's no use discussing her, David. It doesn't help. I'd better start getting ready for the next case. If we're not ready when Mr Morrell returns I shall be in more hot water. But there will be about ten minutes to spare for coffee in the office if I hurry.'

'I'm on my way there now. I'll save you a cup. Don't be too long, Andrea. We never get enough time to chat together. We're all so wrapped up in our own little worlds.'

Andrea nodded and went on with her work. There were so many things to be considered, but of one thing she was certain. She was going to have serious trouble with Sister Cole! Events were shaping towards a climax, and yet there was no reason why there should be trouble between them.

A terrific crash startled her, and she swung round to see Nurse Harmer bending quickly to pick up the tray of dirty instruments which she had dropped on the way to the sterilizer. Nurse Whittaker hurried across to help pick

27

up the instruments, and Andrea caught her breath and prevented a sigh escaping her compressed lips. Sister Cole was not the only one making life a burden! Nurse Harmer was doing her best to make things more awkward and it came to Andrea that perhaps the girl was doing it deliberately just to help Sister Cole in her strange vendetta!

'Sister!' Simon Morrell's harsh voice from the doorway stopped Andrea as she started towards the nurses, and she turned to look at his stiff figure. 'Come here please!'

She glanced at the nurses once more, then moved to the door, and she wondered what had happened to bring him back so quickly. The thought crossed her mind that perhaps at last he was going to ask her out for an evening! She was hopeful for a moment, but then smiled wistfully as she rejected the thought. That was purely wishful thinking. Clifford Stevens was the only man who ever asked her out! It came to her then that she had about as much chance of going out with Simon as Clifford had of dating her, and that seemed to sum up the situation exactly.

'Sister Chaston!' Simon's tones were thin and sharp, his dark eyes were gleaming with anger as she joined him in the corridor outside the theatre. 'I have admired your work in theatre from the first moment we worked together, I don't think I have ever met your equal. But there's just one side of you that doesn't measure up. You're not firm enough with the nurses! I heard that tray of instruments fall just now, and I've no doubt it was Nurse Harmer's fault. That's the second time she's dropped something today. You've got to do something about her! I want her out of the theatre. Is that clearly understood? I refuse to have her around! Get rid of her.'

'I've already spoken to Sister Cole about her, Mr Morrell!' Andrea thrust down her shining hopes, and the very sharpness of his tones was like a scalpel cutting through her heart. He was apparently devoid of the usual emotions controlling most men. He didn't care in the least about women! The knowledge that she would never have any chance with him flared in her mind, and her disappointment was so great that tears came into her eyes. She blinked rapidly and moistened her lips, afraid that he would notice her agitation. But he was already turning away.

'If you can't handle your job then I'll find someone who can.' he said sharply, his dark eyes narrowing as he glanced back over his shoulder at her.

Andrea gasped in shock and horror, and her spirits sank instantly to below zero. She watched him striding away along the corridor. Her nerves seemed to shrink and warp, and a trembling seized hold of her. Oh, Lord, why did life have to be so difficult? She sighed and shook her head slowly. Why couldn't a miracle occur that would smooth out Sister Cole's harsh manner? She searched her thoughts for another factor that would need divine intervention before a change could be wrought, and her mind seemed to freeze as it readily supplied one. Why couldn't Simon Morrell suddenly decide that he loved his theatre Sister? At that moment it was Andrea's greatest wish!

She went along to the office, feeling the need for her coffee, and when she entered, David got to his feet from the chair beside Sister Cole's desk and poured a cup of coffee for her.

'Sit down,' he commanded. 'You look all in. Here!' He handed the coffee to her. 'I don't suppose it will do you much good, but it's better than nothing.'

'Thank you!' Andrea took the cup, but her hands were trembling so much that she could not hold it, and David took it from her and set it down on the desk.

'I'm sure you're sickening for something,' he said slowly studying her pale face. 'You look ghastly, Andrea. Are you feeling ill?'

'I'm all right, David,' she retorted, passing a weary hand before her eyes. 'I've got to get rid of Nurse Harmer. Mr Morrell has just been at me again. I spoke to Sister Cole about it this morning and started more trouble. But this time something will have to be done. I don't know why Sister Cole should stand up for

30

Nurse Harmer the way she does! I know they're friends, but there is a limit to what friendship can do.'

'I'm certainly going to have something to say to Iris Cole about her manner,' he said slowly. 'I couldn't possibly make the situation any worse.'

'It would just inform her that she's really getting through to me,' Andrea said, shaking her head. 'Please don't say anything.'

'All right.' He sighed sharply, shaking his head almost angrily. 'But this can't go on, Andrea, and you know it. You'll finish up with a nervous breakdown.' He drained his cup and got to his feet. 'I'd better get back to work. The next patient is due down in theatre shortly. Drink that coffee like a good girl, and don't worry so much. Let it all go over your head.'

'I'm not the type to be able to do that, but I'll try,' she retorted.

He departed, and Andrea relaxed, her slim shoulders slumping a little. Her head was aching dully, and there was unaccustomed bitterness in her mind. She started nervously when the door of the office was suddenly thrust open, and Nurse Harmer looked in. The girl stared at Andrea for a moment, then came in and shut the door.

'I suppose Mr Morrell wanted to talk to you about me!' Nurse Harmer said. Her voice was filled with sullen defiance.

'What did you expect?' Andrea shook her head. 'I'm tired of the whole business. I suspect you've been deliberately failing in your duty just to get me into trouble in some way. But you've done it for yourself. Mr Morrell says you've got to go. You'll be returned to ward duty when I've had the chance to talk to Sister Cole.'

'We'll see about that! You've got your knife into me! That's the whole trouble. You've never liked me! You're always so right and so clever! It isn't fair!'

Before Andrea could say anything the girl had turned and hurried to the door. Andrea let her go without comment. There was no point in arguing about it. They both knew there was no truth in the girl's accusations. But Sister Cole would believe them, and Andrea wondered just what tales Nurse Harmer had carried to their superior, and suddenly she was sitting bolt-upright, her face showing a frown, her pale green eyes narrowed as she considered. Was that the cause of Sister Cole's harsh manner? Had she been fed with a stream of complaints and tales about Andrea's methods and manner? Was that why she was making life so unpleasant?

The door opened again, and this time Sister Cole herself walked into the office. She stared at Andrea, and if looks could kill Andrea would have been mortally hurt.

'I've just seen Nurse Harmer, and she was

crying. She came out of here. What have you been saying to her?' Sister Cole sailed into the attack immediately, and Andrea felt her nerves tighten once more.

'I've been telling her that Mr Morrell says she's got to go,' Andrea retorted. 'Twice this morning she dropped things. She's worse than a first-year student. I've been threatened myself because of this. If I don't do my job properly then I'll be replaced. Well it's my job to decide if a nurse doesn't fit in with my team, and if she doesn't then she has to go. I'm telling you, Sister, that I can't have Nurse Harmer with me any longer.'

Silence followed, and Andrea found she was clenching her hands and gritting her teeth. She stared into her superior's face, and Sister Cole's brown eyes were narrowed and calculating. But before she could answer there was a knock on the door and it was opened to admit Simon. He paused and looked from Andrea's face to Sister Cole's before coming fully into the office, and then he moved to Sister Cole, standing at her side and looking down at her.

'Has Sister Chaston told you about Nurse Harmer?' he demanded.

'She was just telling me,' came the reluctant reply.

'Well she's got to go. I understand that Sister Chaston has spoken to you before about getting rid of Nurse Harmer and that you overruled her. I don't know what kind of a war is going on between you two, but I won't let it interfere with my work. So make arrangements for Nurse Harmer to be taken out of my sight and theatre or I will see Matron and tell her that neither of you is doing her work properly.'

'Mr Morrell!' Sister Cole seemed about to explode, and Andrea felt that she could not sit through another argument. She got to her feet.

'If you'll excuse me,' she said quickly. 'I must get back to the theatre. I've told Sister Cole that Nurse Harmer must go, so it is up to her, Mr Morrell, and I'd like you to know that I'm quite prepared to report to Matron if you feel I'm not performing my duties to your standards.'

She walked out of the office, her cheeks aflame, and there was a great trembling inside her. She took a deep quivering breath as she went along the corridor to the theatre, and she could feel a ball of emotion swelling in her breast. Her eyes were suddenly filled with scalding tears, and no amount of blinking would bring them under control. David Hewitt appeared from the surgeons' room at that moment, almost as she passed the door, and he paused to avoid bumping into her. Andrea made a great effort to control the tears shimmering in her eyes, and she might have succeeded if David hadn't noticed her distress.

'Andrea, what on earth is wrong?' he demanded sympathetically, and put a hand to her slim shoulder.

The gentleness of his voice seemed to slash through Andrea's control, and she was horrified when she burst into tears and began to cry. She saw David's face through a shimmering mask, and then he had put his arms around her, patting her shoulder to comfort her.

'Come on, Andrea, this isn't like you,' he said gently. 'Don't let them get you down. Show them you don't care.'

She sniffed miserably, trying to regain control of herself, and she knew it wasn't just the trouble with Sister Cole, that was getting at her. It was her love for Simon Morrell, a vain love that was doomed to failure because it had been sown in a barren desert of a man who did not care for anything outside his sphere of surgery.

She heard footsteps along the corridor, and tried to push David away. He was still holding her in his arms, trying to console her, and he was so intent upon her condition that he seemed to forget that they were in the corridor. The next moment Simon passed them quickly and Andrea heard his harsh voice.

'This is not the time or the place for such goings on! David, you ought to know better! And I'm surprised at you, Sister! No wonder the nurses are out of hand when their superiors act like this.'

Andrea closed her eyes, trying to keep the cutting words from wounding her, and she felt David stiffen angrily. She clung to his arms as he turned to say something to Simon, who was still moving swiftly along the corridor.

'Let it pass,' she said wearily! 'It will only make matters worse!'

'I'm damned if I will,' David retorted. 'I'm not going to stand for this a moment longer. If you're willing to let him use you as a doormat, I'm not. I'm going to straighten him out on one or two matters to which he's blind. Sister Cole isn't the only one who can cause trouble if she's of a mind to.'

He turned away quickly and hurried after Simon, and Andrea watched him go while she struggled to regain her composure. She had thought the situation couldn't get worse, but now she was not so sure. She dried her eyes and went on to the theatre, hopeless and confused, and there was a silent prayer in her mind. If only it could be answered!

CHAPTER THREE

Sister Cole appeared in the doorway to the theatre just after Andrea entered, and she was accompanied by Nurse Speldon from her own surgical team. Andrea had recovered her composure by this time, and there was very little trace of the tears she had shed. But she braced herself for trouble, and forced herself to go across to where her superior waited.

'Nurse Speldon is taking Nurse Harmer's place in your team, Sister,' Iris Cole said coldly. Her face was stiff with her efforts to remain expressionless, and although she succeeded in keeping her features from revealing her thoughts, her voice trembled with suppressed emotion.

Andrea nodded, not trusting herself to speak, but she half turned and called to Nurse Harmer, who came across.

'You're working with me in future,' Sister Cole told her friend. 'Come along.' She didn't look at Andrea again, but she spoke quickly. 'Now let us have no more trouble in this theatre or I shall see Matron myself.'

Andrea realized that she had gained some kind of a victory over Sister Cole, but only upon Simon's intervention, and when she realized that David and Simon might get at loggerheads because of what had been said in the corridor she knew her troubles were far from being ended. But she sighed heavily in relief when Nurse Harmer departed with Sister Cole, and she looked at Nurse Speldon with speculation in her pale eyes.

Rita Speldon was a tall, slim blonde with pale blue eyes and a wonderful face and figure. At twenty-five, she had been around the hospital in most of the departments since she'd

37

qualified as a nurse, and she had quite a reputation. She had only to snap her figures to gain the attention of any man, and she had put this advantage to work for her a number of times in the past, sometimes to the detriment of her character. There had been a near scandal with one doctor, who had departed rather hurriedly, and there were always rumours of one kind or another going the rounds about the girl. But she was a first class theatre nurse, and Andrea was happy to have her.

'We're rather pushed for time,' Andrea said. 'Pitch in, Nurse!'

'Right, Sister! Don't worry! I can handle my end of the work. You've been having a lot of trouble with Harmer, but you won't have to supervise me!'

'That will be a relief!' Andrea smiled and eased a sigh from her throat. 'We'll have a chat later, but we're due to start operating very shortly.'

They went about their duties, and Andrea could not help glancing towards the door, wondering what David had said to Simon. When they came into Theatre together, Andrea looked at their faces, but she could not tell by either man's expression what might have passed between them.

Simon came straight towards Andrea, and she stiffened, glad she was wearing her mask, but he looked deeply into her pale eyes, and his own eyes were narrowed and expressionless.

'I'm sorry to tell you, Sister, that after getting you to change your half-day because of the Op this afternoon we shan't be operating. The patient's condition has deteriorated, and I think it will be better to wait for a day or so. You can change back to your original schedule now, I suppose?'

'I don't know. Sister Cole won't be pleased. She didn't want Nurse Harmer to leave our team, but as you see, she's gone now and Nurse Speldon has joined us from Sister Cole's team.'

'Oh good!' His eyes beamed as he looked across the theatre to where Rita Speldon was helping Nurse Whittaker by the sterilizers. 'We're lucky to get her. Great things are expected of her, you know. From what I've heard of her around the hospital, I'd say we're most fortunate to get her.'

Andrea wondered if he'd heard the same stories she had gleaned from the hospital grapevine, but it was none of her business what any of the nurses did when off duty. So long as they worked well on duty, that was all she was concerned with.

Simon went over to speak to Rita Speldon, and Andrea watched them. They were both wearing masks, so she could not even guess at their expressions, but she knew by the way Rita twisted her body into unconscious poses that the girl was a born flirt and could not help attracting men. But she was relieved that Simon had said nothing about the incident in the corridor, and Andrea sighed heavily with relief and went back to work.

The rest of the morning passed off without incident, and Andrea was more than satisfied with the way Rita Speldon did her work. They seemed to get on all the better with the girl in Nurse Harmer's place, and it seemed to Andrea that Simon's harsh tones had mellowed a little. If it was the effect of the new nurse in the team then all the better, Andrea thought as the last case of the morning was wheeled out of the theatre. She had been convinced for some weeks that Nurse Harmer's nagging presence had made Simon much worse than he naturally was.

They began cleaning up, and Andrea left the theatre to go and have a word with Sister Cole. David was coming out of the surgeons' room as she went to her office, and he smiled at her.

'Will you be ready to go home in about twenty minutes?' he demanded. 'I'll drive you home. I'd like to talk to you.'

'Thanks, I'll be ready. I'll see you outside at the car park.' She wanted to ask him how he had got on with Simon, but dared not broach the subject. He walked with her as far as her office door, and patted her shoulder reassuringly as he went on and she entered the

40

office.

Sister Cole was at her desk and Nurse Harmer was seated in the chair beside it. Conversation ceased at Andrea's entrance, and she wondered at their topic as they glanced rather guiltily at her. But Andrea had changed slightly inside during the morning. Events had caused so much pressure in her mind that she instinctively began to resist. She paused by the larger desk where her superior sat and looked down into Iris Cole's dark eyes.

'Mr Morrell has told me that the operation scheduled for this afternoon will not now be performed,' Andrea said. 'I'd like to have the afternoon off as originally listed.'

'I see!' Sister Cole spoke heavily. For a moment it seemed that she would argue about it, but she nodded slowly. 'I don't see why we shouldn't stick to the original roster if possible. All right, take the afternoon off. Make sure your theatre is clean before you go.'

Andrea nodded, slightly exasperated by the reminder to make sure that theatre was clean before going off duty. There was no need for that kind of remark, she knew. But she said nothing, and hardly glanced at Nurse Harmer as she turned and departed.

As soon as the theatre was completely cleaned and prepared for emergency, Andrea went into the locker room and changed into her uniform. She heaved a long sigh of relief as she let her mind relax from the high pinnacle

41

of alertness that was demanded by duty, and she paused when Nurse Speldon came by.

'I shan't be here this afternoon,' Andrea said. 'I don't know what your duties are for the rest of this week, but you'll probably swap duties with Nurse Harmer. However you'd better have a word with Sister Cole about it right away. She's in her office.'

'I'll see her at once, Sister,' the girl replied, and smiled cheerfully as she turned away.

Andrea looked for Nurse Whittaker and explained about the cancelled operation. 'Keep yourself busy this afternoon, because you know what Sister Cole is,' she added. 'I'm going off duty now until tomorrow morning.'

'You must look forward to the times you're off duty, I should think,' Nurse Whittaker retorted, and her red-gold hair glinted under her cap. She had expressive blue eyes, and there was an angry glint in them as she looked into Andrea's face. 'I don't know how you put up with everything. They don't make your life easy for you.'

Andrea smiled. 'I can take it,' she said, glancing at her watch. 'See you tomorrow, I must run now. I'm getting a lift home.'

'Mr Stevens?' the girl demanded.

'No, Mr Hewitt.' Andrea left the theatre and hurried from the department, leaving the hospital and walking into the car park.

David was sitting behind the wheel in his black Jaguar, and he smiled as he got out and walked around to open the front passenger door for her.

'I was about to give you up for lost,' he said. 'But I know you're never finished while you're on duty.' He closed the door on her when she was seated in the car, and walked around to his seat. Andrea, looking around the park, saw Simon getting into his white Fiat, and she knew he had seen her get into David's car, although he didn't appear to look in their direction. 'Well,' David continued as he drove out of the park. 'What a morning it has been, to be sure. But I think I've helped clear the air a bit.'

'With Mr Morrell, do you mean?'

'I had a few words with him! I don't know what makes that man tick! He's little better than Iris Cole, you know. He doesn't say much, I grant you. But he's almost anti-social, you know! I've asked him out for a drink once or twice, but he won't accept. In the three months that he's been here I've never heard that he's been out to enjoy himself, and he certainly hasn't got a girl friend.'

Andrea didn't want to interrupt him while he was talking about Simon, and she listened intently. Her heart seemed to miss a beat when she learned that Simon apparently didn't have a girl friend.

'There must be something wrong with a man who doesn't ever relax or get out and about. He's only about thirty-two! Now is the time for him to enjoy himself. I rather fancy he had some trouble at his last place, and that is why he came to us. I know someone at the hospital where he last worked. I'll get in touch and try to get some information about our dear Mr Morrell.'

'What did you say to him this morning?' Andrea demanded.

'I told him just what happened. He said he hadn't noticed that Sister Cole had been giving you a hard time of it lately. That proves he doesn't care what goes on about him! But he apologised for what he said, and was going to apologise to you personally, but I told him I'd tell you. Perhaps he isn't a bad sort after all! But it wouldn't hurt him to be a bit more human where we're concerned.'

Andrea sighed slowly, her mind filled with the events of the morning. But she was feeling easier now. Nurse Harmer was gone from the team and she felt that the girl had been the main cause for the trouble she'd been getting from Sister Cole. But her superior would find out what kind of a nurse Janet Harmer was!

The streets of Surlington were crowded with lunch-hour traffic, and David concentrated upon his driving. They went through the town centre and he drove on to the outskirts where Andrea lived with her parents. She was content to relax now, and her mind rested until David reached her home and turned into the driveway.

'Asleep?' he demanded, glancing at her as the car followed the winding drive under an avenue of tall beech and oak trees.

'Very nearly,' she replied, smiling as she stirred. The house, a tall, square building with a grey slate roof and its walls hidden beneath a thick covering of green creeper, slid into view as David turned the last bend and then brought the car to a halt on the gravel spread before the building.

'I suppose you'll lie out on the lawn all afternoon,' he went on. 'You look as if you could do with some sun on you. What do you do with yourself when you're off duty, Andrea? You don't appear to have any friends! I've been leading off about Simon Morrell being anti-social, but you're another who remains aloof from the rest of the world.'

'I lead a full life,' she replied, opening the car door. 'Thanks for the lift, David. See you tomorrow!'

'Okay!' He smiled and nodded and she slammed the door. He lifted a hand and turned the car, and Andrea stood watching him until he had gone around the nearest bend in the drive.

Silence came down after the sound of his car faded, and Andrea stood motionless for long moments. She was still uncoiling inside, like a spring that had been wound too tightly. She looked around the familiar garden, with its smooth lawns and coloured flower beds, and she caught sight of movement beyond the standard roses that lined the crazy-paved path leading to the greenhouses. The next moment her mother stepped into view, waving a greeting, and Andrea smiled and waved in reply, then went along the path to meet the older woman.

'Hello, Andrea, you're early!' Mary Chaston was not as tall as her daughter, and she had pale grey eyes and fair hair. At fifty-three she was beginning to show faint signs of getting old, but there was a youthful bloom to her cheeks and a vivaciousness about her that was all too evident.

'David drove me home or I would still be waiting for a bus,' Andrea replied. 'Isn't it too hot for getting out into the garden?'

'The weeds won't wait for cooler weather. I'll come in and get your lunch for you. It's Millie's afternoon off and she's gone to the swimming pool.'

'Good for Millie!' Andrea tried to sound relaxed and at ease, but she could hear strain in her tones, and hoped her mother wouldn't notice. 'I can get my own lunch!'

'I'll get it for you. You must be tired after working all morning. I want to talk to you, anyway. I'm not quite happy about the way you're looking these days.'

'What do you mean?' Andrea turned and started towards the house and her mother fell into step at her side. 'Am I looking any different?'

'You're looking very strained and unwell!' There was a severe note in Mary Chaston's voice. 'Perhaps you forget that I was a nursing Sister before I married your father. You can't fool me, Andrea. Something is wrong, probably at the hospital, and I feel that you ought to tell me about it.'

'Oh, it's nothing very much. My superior has her knife into me for some unknown reason, and she's made life a bit hectic. But I have the feeling the situation will improve now. There was a change made this morning and it was for the better.'

'If that's all it is then I'll mind my own business, but I was beginning to think it was something else.' Mrs Chaston kept her tones even and controlled as they entered the house and went through to the kitchen.

'Something else?' Andrea glanced into her mother's pale eyes, shaking her head as if mystified. 'What else could there be? I don't have a care in the world.'

'I thought perhaps you'd made friends with some handsome doctor at the hospital and that love was affecting you.'

'Love!' Andrea shook her head. 'I'm too busy when I'm on duty to have time to think of anything but the cases we handle. Anyway, I'm not the type to fall in love.'

'You've changed a lot in the past ten years!'

'I've got ten years older. I hope I've

47

matured correctly.' A smile touched the corners of Andrea's mouth. She looked her mother in the eyes. 'You can stop worrying about me. This morning we cleared the air, so to speak. There's nothing else to worry about'.

Mrs Chaston nodded, and set about getting Andrea's meal for her. Andrea didn't feel in the least hungry, but she ate the meal to please her mother. She was relieved when her mother went back to the garden, and after she had cleaned the kitchen she went up to her room to get out of uniform.

Taking a shower, Andrea closed her eyes and let the thrumming streams of water strike her body. She used hot water at first, then cooled it until her body seemed to vibrate under the powerful jets. Then she towelled herself briskly and dressed in a black skirt and a white frilled blouse. She pushed her feet into green mules and felt completely relaxed.

She had got out of the habit of looking into the future. In the back of her mind was the ever present wish that Simon would suddenly take notice of her, that he might overnight lose his frigid manner and become friendly. But she had given up all hope of it ever happening, and this afternoon she suddenly felt the desire to get out of the usual routine and do something that was completely out of character. She thought of the things she might do, and shook her head. She didn't want to help in the garden or go to the library to change the books. There had to be something else which would help her get out of the depths into which she had fallen.

Acting upon an impulse, she put on sandals and went down into the garden to where her mother was working on the roses.

'You're looking better,' Mrs Chaston said, eyeing her closely.

'I feel better. I'm going out for the afternoon, Mother. I don't know if I'll come back to tea, but I have an appointment with Father at four-thirty for my six-monthly check-up.'

'He did mention it,' Mrs Chaston retorted. 'Ring him before you go out and tell him you'll be along to see him. 'If you're going into the town centre will you change the library books? It will save me having to turn out. Take the car if you wish.'

'Thanks, but I'd rather use the bus. There's hardly ever a parking place for a car these days. I'll change the books for you.'

'Thank you. Have a nice time.' Mrs Chaston returned to her work, and Andrea shook her head ruefully and turned away.

Collecting the library books, Andrea left the house and started down the drive. Then she remembered that she hadn't called her father and she returned to the house. Dialling a number, she heard an efficient female voice at the other end reply with the usual phrase, and she smiled as she gave her name.

'Please tell my father I'll be in at four-thirty

for my check-up, Nancy.'

'Andrea! Yes, of course. I'll look forward to seeing you.' The dental receptionist sounded as if she wanted to chat, but Andrea was impatient to depart.

'I'll see you at four-thirty,' she cut in, and replaced the receiver.

Catching a bus at the end of the road, Andrea went into the town centre. She had plenty of time, and went into the library to change the books. Her mother liked nurse and doctor romances, and Andrea browsed through the shelves, reading passages from some of the novels and wishing that real hospital life was as rosy as that painted by the fiction writers.

'I don't believe it!' The male voice was at her elbow, and Andrea looked up quickly to see Simon Morrell standing beside her.

She firmed her lips as her heart seemed to lurch at the sight of him. He was smiling thinly, dressed in a cream, open-neck shirt and fawn trousers, with highly polished brown shoes on his feet.

'I was coming out of the Reference Section when I saw you coming in to change your books,' he went on. But don't tell me you read nurse and doctor stories!' He was looking at the cover of the book she was holding.

Andrea flushed despite her control, and she forced a smile.

'My mother was a nursing Sister before she

50

married, and I suppose she feels nostalgic. No doubt this type of book takes her back to when she was young.'

'Do you do much reading?'

'I'm usually too tired when I get off duty to read. I like reading, but these days when I sit down with a good book I usually fall asleep. You don't read fiction, do you? I wouldn't say you're the type.'

He smiled and glanced down at the three books under his arm.

'What type am I?' he countered.

She took a deep breath, feeling strange and awkward in his presence. She had never seen him away from the hospital. And it was the first time she'd seen him out of hospital whites. He looked even more handsome, casually dressed, and the harshness that held his expression around the hospital was gone now. She was surprised to see him smile, and that was something else she had never seen him do before.

'I don't know anything at all about you,' she said.

'But we've worked together for three months.'

She nodded slowly, thinking of all the times they had stood for hours within a few feet of one another. She suppressed a sigh and shook her head.

'You're the best surgeon I've ever worked with,' she told him.

'Don't let Sir Humphrey hear you say that,' he retorted, but he seemed quite pleased with her words. 'I'd like to talk to you. We never get the time to chat at the hospital, and I wouldn't ask you out for fear of starting rumours and gossip around the hospital. What are your plans for this afternoon?'

'I have a dental appointment at my father's surgery at four-thirty, but I've got nothing to do until then.'

'Would you care to have tea with me until then?' He glanced at his watch. 'I've been thinking about you ever since this morning, and although David said he would apologise for me I've felt that I ought to do my own apologising. I was rather rude to you this morning, and the fact that I didn't know what it was all about is no excuse.'

Andrea was staring into his face, unable to believe that this was taking place. They had met off duty and he was actually asking her to have tea with him. She felt like crying, and fought down her emotions. What would he think of her if she burst into tears because he'd asked her to spend some time with him? She smiled at the thought and nodded.

'I was just thinking that a cup of tea would be very nice right now,' she told him.

'Fine! Have you selected the books you want? Don't let me hurry you!' A smile touched his lips, changing his face completely. He looked a lot younger when he wasn't

52

serious, and Andrea felt her pulses begin to race. 'I'm afraid I spend most of my working life chasing you around. You must hate the sight of me!'

'I have a great deal of respect for you.' She chose her words carefully.

'I feel the same way about you,' he retorted, smiling again, and Andrea had to turn to the book shelf to hide her expression from him. She couldn't see the titles on the books as she looked at them, and she picked three at random, hoping her mother hadn't read them before. 'I'll carry them for you,' he went on when she turned back to him, and she trembled as their fingers touched momentarily. He took the books and they walked to the check-out.

When they were in the street, Andrea took a deep breath and felt her soul expand with pleasure. This was how an imprisoned bird must feel when it found liberty again, she thought, and she kept looking up into his face just to convince herself that this was no dream. It wouldn't have been the first time she had dreamed about him, she reminded herself. But this time it was real, and she began to hope that Fate had taken a hand at last in her affairs. But whatever was behind this unexpected coming together, she was going to make the most of it, and she matched him stride for stride as they went along the pavement, her mind soaring and her thoughts happier than they had been for a very long time.

CHAPTER FOUR

Time passed so quickly in Simon's company that Andrea felt that no sooner had they sat down in the cafe with a pot of tea between them than she had to consider going for her dental appointment. But in the hours they spent together she listened avidly to what Simon had to say and also said quite a lot herself, once she had overcome her initial surprise at being with him. She delayed as long as possible her departure, but finally she had to draw his attention to the time, and he apologized immediately.

'I am sorry. Where is your father's surgery?'

'It's only ten minutes from here.' She smiled.

'I have to get myself fixed up with a dentist,' he went on. 'I suppose you recommend your father!' A smile touched his face, and Andrea nodded quickly. 'Then perhaps I may walk with you to your father's surgery and find out if he will take me on his panel of patients. I like to have a six-monthly check-up, and I've been here three months without seeing a dentist.'

She nodded eagerly as they arose from the

54

table, and Andrea felt as if she were walking on air when they went out into the sunlight and walked the hot pavements. She thought of all the times they had worked together, and of the nights when she had dreamed of being out with him. A wistfulness touched her and she knew this moment would not last forever. Then tomorrow they would meet again at the hospital and all would be the same as before.

But she pushed all those thoughts into the back of her mind. Let tomorrow take care of itself! One had to live in the present if one was going to get the best from life. She thought of her mother's advice, and smiled.

'You're a very serious man on duty,' she observed as they went on.

'We have a very serious profession on our hands!'

'I know. No one takes nursing more seriously than I! But I sense there's more to it with you.'

'You're very observant. But aren't there any rumours about me going the rounds of the hospital?'

'I haven't heard anything.'

'And I imagine you're not the kind of girl who would listen to that sort of thing.'

'Thank you!' She smiled as she spoke, and their glances met. He seemed very serious now, and his brown eyes held a measure of sadness in their dark depths. She wondered if he had been crossed in love. Perhaps that was what was wrong with him! The more she thought about it the more likely it seemed to be the right answer. But if that was the case then he would get over it eventually, and the fact that he had bothered to speak to her when he needn't have made his presence known to her made her feel confident that at some time in the future he might ask her out for an evening.

It was on the stroke of four-thirty when they entered her father's surgery, and the receptionist greeted them.

'Mr Chaston is waiting for you, Andrea!'

'Thank you, Nancy! Come along, Simon!' She paused and looked into his face, for it was the first time she had used his name. He studied her for a moment, then smiled.

'What's wrong? My name is Simon, you know.'

'It seems so strange after three months of calling you Mr Morrell!' Andrea glanced at the receptionist and saw the puzzlement on the girl's face. She quickly explained the situation and then led Simon into her father's surgery. 'Father, I want you to meet Simon Morrell, one of the surgeons at the hospital,' she said quickly. 'He's been with us only for three months and he hasn't fixed himself up with a dentist yet. Will you take care of him?'

Henry Chaston was a tall, powerful man in his middle fifties, and his blue eyes gleamed as he came forward with outstretched hand.

'How do you do, Simon?' I believe we have met before. Weren't you at Sir Humphrey Ruddle's do the other week?'

'Yes, I was,' Simon replied. 'I remember you quite well, but I didn't know you were Andrea's father.'

'I didn't know you were friendly with my daughter. I would have asked you round to the house if I had known. You must have thought me inhospitable!'

'Not at all! Andrea and I are not exactly friends. She's my theatre Sister! I bumped into her at the library this afternoon and we went for a cup of tea. I didn't even know her father was a dental surgeon until she told me this afternoon.'

'I'll check on your mouth after I've examined Andrea,' Henry Chaston said. 'Sit in the chair, Andrea.'

Andrea was trembling with suppressed excitement, and she was also sorry that she had declined an invitation to attend Sir Humphrey's party two weeks before. Her parents had attended but she had felt too tired after a full and heavy day in Theatre. She got into the chair and relaxed, and listened to her father's conversation with Simon while her mouth was examined. Then it was Simon's turn, and he got into the chair in her place, smiling at her as he did so.

'You really must come to the house when you have an evening free,' Henry Chaston said as he examined Simon. 'Have you made any friends in the time that you've been in Surlington?'

'Not really! I'm always very busy, and to tell you the truth I don't make friends very easily. I suppose the real trouble is that I'm inclined to be shy. It's something I've always had to fight against.'

'Well Andrea is just the girl to help you over that, I should think,' her father said. 'She's never been a girl to mix a lot, but I don't think it's shyness with her. She likes to be on her own.'

'You'll say that I'm not normal before you've finished discussing me,' she interposed, and her father chuckled, his blue eyes alive with delight as he glanced at her.

'You're normal, as far as I can tell, but your mother is worried about you because you never show any interest in the opposite sex. I don't think it's serious. Probably lack of opportunity. The job you do ties you down a great deal, but you are twenty-nine now, and next year they'll be calling you an old maid!'

Simon chuckled, and Andrea breathed deeply as her pleasure swelled.

'Just call in my assistant,' Henry Chaston went on. 'You have two fillings that need renewing, Simon. I'll do them now if you wish.'

'Please do!' Simon retorted.

Andrea called in her father's nurse, and she stood in the background while Simon was attended to. Ten minutes later they were both ready to leave.

'What are you doing this evening?' Henry Chaston demanded. 'I know that Andrea is off duty, so I expect you must be, too. Would you care to join us at home? That's if you haven't made any other arrangements!'

'I've got nothing to do,' Simon said. 'I went to the library this afternoon to get some books to read later. But I can always read. I don't get asked out too often, so I make a point of accepting any invitations.'

'Good. Andrea, why don't you call your mother now and tell her about Simon? Then take him home with you! I can remember when I was very young and alone in a big town. It is difficult to make friends, surprising as it may seem. I know I was always thankful for any helping hand that was offered to me.'

'It's very kind of you, but I wouldn't want to push myself upon Andrea,' Simon said, looking at her. 'Perhaps she's made other arrangements for this evening.'

'Not Andrea,' her father said.

'I haven't,' she agreed. 'I would have sat and read one of these hospital romances! Perhaps I might have learned something from them. But I'll take you home with me, Simon. Mother was a nursing Sister, as I told you, and she'll be delighted to meet you.'

Henry Chaston glanced at his watch and nodded. 'I'm sorry I must chase you away now,

59

but I have another patient due, and the duty calls. But I'll see you later, Simon, and it's been a pleasure to meet you again.'

'Thank you, Mr Chaston,' Simon replied, and he took Andrea's arm as they left the surgery.

Andrea almost stumbled as she felt Simon's fingers close upon her elbow. She caught her breath and felt her pulses begin to race. All her deepest dreams seemed to be coming true, and she could have thrown herself into her father's arms in appreciation for what he had done. But for him she and Simon might have parted upon leaving the surgery, but now she knew he would be in her company at least for the better part of the evening.

'I've got a car somewhere,' Simon said as they went out to the street. He paused and considered for a moment. 'We'll have to walk to it.' He still held her arm as he looked down into her face, and Andrea was certain that he must be able to read her joy in her eyes. 'It's certainly a small world, isn't it? I remember meeting your father at Sir Humphrey's party, and he impressed me a great deal. I didn't know he was your father. I wonder if your mother will remember me?'

'I'm sure she will! She wouldn't forget a man as handsome as you.' Andrea's eyes sparkled, and he shook her gently as he grinned.

'I can hardly believe all this,' he said as they walked on. 'I keep thinking of you as I see you around the hospital. I've worked with you for three months, and I never really knew you. You're not at all what I expected you to be.'

'Oh!' She looked into his dark eyes. 'Is that a compliment or the opposite?'

'I've got the highest possible opinion of you,' he countered.

'As far as my duties and status as a Sister go! But there's much more to a nurse than the way she handles herself at the hospital.'

'I'm afraid I'm inclined to forget that sometimes.' His face was tensing a little, and she noticed.

'I've told myself that often,' she admitted.

'You think I haven't noticed that you're a human, a woman beneath your uniform?' He smiled now, and his eyes were bright. 'I've noticed all right. The knowledge has been most disturbing at times.'

'Really?' She frowned as she looked intently at him. 'That's a strange thing to say.'

He didn't answer, and she wisely decided to drop the subject. But he still held her arm as they walked on, and when they reached his car she stood watching him while he unlocked the doors. Then she got in at his side, and their shoulders brushed and she set her teeth as strange emotions filled her and set her teeth on edge and started her nerves jumping. She almost turned to him with the intention of pushing herself into his arms, and had to fight hard against the impulse. But it warned her just how powerful her emotions were. She knew she would have to be careful and give this pleasant situation time to grow naturally.

She found it difficult to believe that they were together at last! She was actually seated in his car, and when she thought of the times she had seen him driving out of the hospital car park and wished she were at his side she could scarcely contain her joy.

She was actually sorry when they reached her home, but there was a pleasure pulse throbbing in her throat. Mrs Chaston was still in the garden, and she came towards them, peeling off her rubber gloves, as they alighted from the car.

'It's Mr Morrell, isn't it?' There was a welcoming smile on Mrs Chaston's face. 'I remember you from Sir Humphrey Ruddle's party.'

'I'm complimented that you should remember me,' he declared, his face showing pleasure.

'Well I can see that I don't have to introduce you two,' Andrea said cheerfully. 'It's a small world, isn't it?' She went on to explain exactly how Simon fitted into her life at the hospital, and by the time she had finished explaining the circumstances of the afternoon there was a jolly atmosphere surrounding them.

'You're the first man Andrea has ever brought home, Simon,' Mrs Chaston said.

'Then I feel honoured,' he retorted,

glancing into Andrea's bright green eyes.

'You'll be thinking there's something psychologically wrong with me,' she returned, 'after listening to what Father had to say about me at his surgery.'

They went into the house and Andrea entertained Simon until her mother had changed. They had tea together, and afterwards walked around the extensive gardens, waiting for Henry Chaston to come home. Andrea felt that she had slipped into a rose-tinted dream, that she was living out the wishes that had haunted her from the moment Simon had appeared at St Catharine's. And she was afraid that suddenly would come the grim awakening, that she would find it was nothing but a dream and that everything was starkly normal.

However the evening was a great success. The only regret Andrea had was that it seemed to pass so quickly. Her father came home and they had dinner. Afterwards they chatted, and Andrea listened intently whenever Simon spoke of his past. His home was in Cornwall, where his parents lived on the coast and his only brother was a doctor in general practice. That was about all she learned of him during the evening, and when it was finally time for him to go she was delighted when her father invited Simon to call at any time. Simon accepted, and Andrea was filled with elation as she went to the door with him.

They went outside into the starlit evening, and the cool breeze was scented by the perfume of the flower beds. Simon's face was just a pale blur in the shadows as he faced her, and Andrea was glad that her own happy expression was concealed from his sharp brown eyes.

'I can safely say that this is the first time I've really enjoyed myself since I came to Surlington,' he said softly. 'And I've learned more about you today than I ever picked up in the previous three months. You're not at all like I imagined you to be, Andrea.'

She thrilled to the sound of her name on his lips, and longed to reach out and touch him, but she controlled her impulses and stood watching him, hoping the pleasures of the day would never fade. He seemed reluctant to go, and she wished that time could stand still for ever. She wanted nothing more from life than to be in his company. But he began to turn away, and she hoped desperately that he would suggest another meeting when they were once more off duty.

'I'll see you at the hospital tomorrow,' he said. 'We have that major operation to perform when the patient is ready for it. I'm hoping it will be tomorrow. The longer we have to wait the less our chances of success. Goodnight, Andrea, and thank you for spending so much time with me today.'

'It made quite a change for me,' she replied, wondering just how bold she dared be. But he went quickly, getting into his car and driving away swiftly.

She stood by the house watching the tail lights of the car disappearing around the bend in the drive, and a great sigh escaped her and she shivered as if an icy wind had blasted the air about her. She took a deep breath and tried to contain all the emotions that had broken loose in her mind, and she felt a thread of anticipation begin to unwind in her thoughts. There was always tomorrow! The ice had been broken and that meant their relationship would begin to change imperceptibly. After a time Simon would begin to look upon her as a friend, and if he came to the house a few more times then he might feel certain processes start their inexorable spasms of birth. It was within the bounds of probability that today had seen the commencement of the realization of Andrea's greatest wish. She mentally crossed her fingers as she went slowly back into the house and prepared to go to bed. For her the age of miracles was not past . . .

Next morning when she first opened her eyes she wondered if she had dreamed of all the wonderful things that had happened the day before, and she had to think hard before she could accept that they were fact. She dressed quickly in her uniform and went down to breakfast, humming a little to herself as she said good morning to the maid, and then ate her breakfast. Then she hurried to catch her bus, and she arrived at the hospital just as David was getting out of his car.

Waiting for him by the entrance, Andrea searched the park for signs of Simon's car, but it hadn't yet arrived, and she smiled to herself as she let her mind ring out with the happy thoughts of the previous day.

'I must say you're looking a lot better this morning,' David commented when he came level with her. 'Your rest has done you good, Andrea. But you're going to have to make up your mind that you won't let Sister Cole worry you any more. I thought you were heading for a nervous breakdown yesterday.'

'Don't worry about me,' Andrea retorted with a smile, and her tones were lofty, filled with elation. 'I've come to terms with myself since yesterday,' she hastened to explain. 'Sister Cole can do what she likes in future. She won't bother me.'

'That's the spirit!' He nodded. 'But I'm not going to let matters rest where they are. You've had a rough time for some weeks now and I want to dig down to get the reasons why.'

'It's better to let sleeping dogs lie,' she pointed out.

'Our particular dog isn't sleeping,' he retorted.

They entered the hospital and walked along the corridors to the department. They parted at the door of the office, and Andrea entered to find Sister Cole seated at her desk.

'Good morning,' Andrea said brightly, and saw surprize show briefly on her superior's set features.

'What's good about it?' came the dragging reply, and for a moment Andrea felt daunted. But she had decided upon using a different attitude towards Iris Cole, and she smiled again as she sat down at her desk and turned her head to look at the Sister.

'Don't you ever feel that it's good to be alive, Sister?' she demanded.

'I've got too much responsibility to be able to spare any thought for things that lay outside of duty. I have to do your work as well as my own.'

'Surely not!' Andrea could feel the old defensiveness seeping back into her mind, and she tried to fight it off. 'What's happened now?'

'I had to go around your theatre after you went off duty yesterday and do several things that were left. It isn't good enough. I have quite enough to do running the department and doing my share of operations without having to chase you up all the time. You're supposed to be my Assistant in this department, but you are more of a hindrance than a help.'

Andrea felt tension rising inside her, but she fought it down. She had resolved never to rise to the bait that Sister Cole always dangled in front of her. She was going to let her superior know that nothing would ever give her cause for worry again. It might take a time for this new attitude to make itself apparent to Sister Cole, but the woman would get the message and then she would have to ease off.

'I've always thought I did my fair share of the extra duties,' Andrea said, 'but if you're working too hard or finding it too difficult to cope then I'll gladly take over more of the work.'

Sister Cole looked as if she would explode, but Andrea smiled disarmingly. Then there was a knock at the door and it opened. Simon stuck his head around the door, looked first at Sister Cole, then saw Andrea.

'Good morning,' he said quietly. His eyes remained on Andrea's face. 'We have a heavy list today, but we must do that major Op which was cancelled yesterday. Shall we try to start earlier than scheduled now in order to make time?'

'Certainly!' Andrea started to her feet. She saw that he was looking worried, and he was in a hurry. He had a clipboard in one hand, and a sheaf of papers clutched to it. He nodded, smiled briefly and hurried out.

Andrea glanced at Sister Cole as she went to the door, but her superior was looking at the papers piled before her. Shaking her head, Andrea departed. She went into the corridor, looking ahead to see Simon passing Nurse Speldon, who was on her way to the theatre, and something white slipped from Simon's papers and fell to the ground ahead of the nurse. Simon turned off into the Surgeon's room and Nurse Speldon picked up the paper.

A frown touched Andrea's face as the nurse glanced at the object which she'd picked up then hurried on to the Nurses' changing room without stopping to give it back to Simon. Setting off in pursuit, Andrea followed the girl. Nurse Speldon went into the room and the door banged at her back. Andrea was breathless by the time she reached the door of the room, and she paused for a moment to regain control of herself. Then she opened the door and entered the room, a gasp escaping from her when she saw Nurse Speldon standing by a locker and hurriedly scanning a letter which she had taken from an envelope. The girl looked guiltily at Andrea, and put her hands behind her back.

'What on earth are you doing, Nurse?' Andrea demanded. 'Is that the letter Mr Morrell dropped?'

'What letter?' came the startled reply.

Andrea explained what she had seen in the corridor, and she held out her hand for the letter. Nurse Speldon stared at her for a moment, then handed the letter and the envelope over.

'I'm interested in Mr Morrell,' the girl said

69

slowly. 'I was only looking to see if the letter was from a girl friend or not.'

'Of all the nerve!' Andrea shook her head sharply. 'I didn't think you'd do such a thing, Nurse!'

'Well I did right by looking,' came the sullen reply. 'I was going to set my cap at Simon Morrell. He's a good catch. But that letter is from a girl. She's his fiancée. She's a nursing Sister and from what she says in that letter she's coming here to work—right in this department!'

Andrea could not prevent shock from showing in her face, and she turned to leave the room, the letter in one hand and the envelope in the other. The letter was open in her hand, just as Nurse Speldon had handed it over, and she didn't realize that Simon was in the corridor until he stopped in front of her.

'I dropped something in the corridor just now,' he said abruptly. 'Have you seen it?' His eyes went to her hands, and Andrea gradually got his face into focus. She saw a frown touch his handsome face, and looked down at the objects in her hands. 'That is my letter,' he said tightly. 'And you've been reading it!' He snatched both letter and envelope from her cold hands, his eyes blazing with anger, and for a moment she thought she saw revulsion and hatred in his cold gaze.

'How dare you accuse me of such a thing?' She was hardly aware of what she was saying,

70

and before she could prevent the impulse she had lifted her hand and slapped his face.

Simon stared at her for a moment, shock in his gaze, and then his lips tightened and he turned and hurried back into his room . . .

CHAPTER FIVE

Andrea stood frozen for some moments, her mind almost blank in shock. She was mortified at what she had done, and her first instinct was to hurry after Simon and apologize for slapping him. But her mind was reeling under the blow that Nurse Speldon had dealt her. Simon had a fiancée, a girl who was coming to St. Catharine's to work!

'Are you all right, Sister?' a voice asked at her side, and Andrea shook herself from the paralysis that seemed to grip her and looked into the concerned face of Nurse Whittaker.

'Yes, thank you, Nurse. I was just thinking about today. We have that major Op to fit in somewhere, and our list for today is rather full.'

'Then we'd better hurry up and get the theatre ready,' the girl said. 'Is Nurse Speldon here yet?'

'Yes, she's in the locker room.' Andrea turned away and forced her mind to concentrate upon what she had to do. Duty

71

came first and she went to prepare to enter Theatre. Once there she soon threw herself into her work, and although she was dreading facing Simon again she had already made up her mind to apologize to him the instant they met.

The nurses came into the theatre and started working, and Nurse Speldon refused to meet Andrea's eyes. Soon the first patient would be brought down, and Andrea kept looking towards the doors, afraid that Simon would arrive, dreading the moment when she would have to speak to him.

When he came into Theatre with the RSO, Andrea steeled herself. But he didn't look in her direction, and she felt her spirits sink as he went into the anteroom to scrub. When he reappeared she was through checking everything and her trolleys were laid up and ready for the first case. She went towards him, hoping no one else would approach him for a moment. He saw her coming and paused, and Andrea was relieved that her mask covered most of her face.

'I want to apologize, Mr Morrell,' she said.

'Apologize?' His mind didn't seem to be on her.

'For slapping you in the corridor!'

'I expect I asked for it. I made a rather nasty accusation against you, and I'm sorry for it. I know you're not a girl like that. Let's call it even, shall we, and forget all about it?'

'Oh yes!' Her voice tremored, and he nodded.

'All right, so it's forgotten. Now let's get to work!'

Andrea nodded and turned away, filled with small relief which slowly died as she realized that although personally they would still be friends, he had a fiancee! She almost choked as she considered. Of course a man as handsome as Simon Morrell would have a woman somewhere in the background of his life. But if only she had known that when he first arrived at the hospital! She wouldn't have fallen in love with him.

The day turned into a nightmare, and how they got through the morning Andrea could hardly recall. The afternoon was as bad! The hours seemed to drag, the heat in the Theatre was terrific, and nothing seemed to go right. Simon was gruff with his commands and instructions, and he hardly spoke apart from uttering the commonplace phrases connected with their work. He couldn't meet Andrea's gaze, she noted with sickening realization, and he snapped at the nurses several times.

They postponed some minor operations to handle the major one which had been cancelled the day before, and it was later than usual when they finally finished for the day. Andrea was on first call, in case of emergency, and she went to her office and sank down in the chair behind her desk when everything was finished. She was utterly drained of strength and felt exhausted. Her head ached and her mind was filled with turmoil. The knowledge that Simon was engaged fought with her emotions, and she realized just how hopeless her love was.

A knock at the door startled her, and she called out an invitation to enter. She was surprised to see Simon when the door opened, and he came slowly into the office, watching her face intently, not sure of himself, and when she remembered his strangeness all day and how he had snapped and almost bullied everyone, she almost broke down and cried.

'Do you mind if I sit down?' he demanded, and dropped into a seat without waiting for her reply. 'What a perfectly rotten day it's been!' he commented harshly, putting a hand to his eyes.

'Would you like some coffee?' she asked. 'I can make some in the kitchen.'

'You're spoiling me,' he retorted, taking his hand away from his eyes and smiling at her. She could see strain and weariness in his expression, and pushed herself to her feet.

'I could do with a cup of coffee myself. It won't take a moment. I'll soon make it.' She started towards the annexe, but he called to her.

'I'd rather take you to a restaurant, if you wouldn't mind,' he said. 'You're as played out as I am, and I want to talk to you. I've got to

74

apologize for what happened in the corridor this morning.'

'You've got to apologize!'

'Of course! I accused you of reading my letter!' He watched her intently.

'I slapped your face,' she said quietly.

'And a good thing too! It put me in my place.' He smiled tightly. 'I certainly asked for it. But I was under considerable pressure when I made that accusation. I could have bitten off my tongue after I said it.'

'I would rather have died than slapped you,' she admitted. She could feel tears stinging her eyes, and turned to the kitchen quickly. She wouldn't break down, whether from relief or anything else, but she was hurt right through to the core by the knowledge that he had a fiancée. There was nothing she could do about that. But the worst fact of all was that the girl was coming here to work. That meant Andrea would see them together, and she knew she would never be able to face that prospect.

She made coffee, and when she took it back into the office on a tray she saw that he was asleep in his chair, one elbow resting on Sister Cole's desk and propping up his head. She paused for a moment, and her heart went out to him. He worked so hard! So much depended upon his efforts and skill. But he didn't seem happy, even though his fiancée was coming here to be with him! The thought crossed her mind as she poured his coffee and then went across to him. She touched his shoulder and he jerked awake instantly, blinking, looked at her with startled brown eyes.

'Oh!' He smiled gently. 'Thank you! What an understanding Sister you are!' He took the cup and saucer and set it down carefully upon the desk. 'Isn't it strange how things can change so drastically and so quickly?'

'How do you mean?' Andrea returned to her seat with her coffee, and she relaxed in her chair and looked at him, trying to keep her emotions dormant.

'Yesterday was the best day I'd ever spent here in three months,' he went on softly. 'I'd been hoping that somehow I could get to know you. I've been so lonely, and I wouldn't make friends with anyone else. But you seemed to be the kind of girl a man could get friendly with and not have any complications arising because of it. Then yesterday we met right out of the blue and I seemed to slip into a place in your scheme of things. I was so happy last night when I left you at your home. I thought I was in with no trouble at all. Then today the sky caves in on me and I'm worse off than I've ever been. I sometimes think that I'm not fated to know happiness.'

'What's wrong?' she demanded. 'Is there anything I can help with?'

'You never think of yourself, do you?' He smiled gently. 'I have noticed that about you.

76

Everyone else comes before you. But there's nothing you can do for me, Andrea. I've got to do it myself. That's why I was such a bully today. I've been trying to reach the hardest decision of my life.'

Andrea said nothing, but she listened intently, and wondered what was coming next. He seemed about to go on, but then he shook his head and began to drink his coffee. She watched him closely, seeing the torment that was in his eyes, and she wished there was something she could do to help. He sighed heavily. He seemed to be in the depths of despair, and his eyes showed the torment that was rife inside him.

'What's wrong?' she asked softly. Recalling Nurse Speldon's words after reading his letter, she thought he ought to be the happiest man in the world because his fiancée was coming to work at the same hospital with him.

'I've decided to leave St. Catherine's,' he said miserably.

'Leave St. Catherine's!' The words were torn from Andrea's heart, and then she was speechless in astonishment. She stared at his face, telling herself that this was a bad dream, and a host of questions rose up in her agile mind.

'I don't want to bother you with my tales of woe,' he said in controlled tones. 'Look, it's been a hard day. I think I'd better go home. How long will you stay here?'

'Until about ten! Then I'll go home.'

'You put in a lot of hours, don't you?'

'It's my job,' She spoke harshly, trying to control her emotions. There was so much she wanted to say to him, but the words would not come. He had a fiancée, and therefore she had no right to try and fill the obvious gap in his life. The attitude which had existed between them the previous day no longer applied, and she knew she now had to try and control her feelings and then kill them. There was nothing more hopeless than loving someone who was already engaged to be married.

'Good night, Andrea.'

She dragged herself from her thoughts to see him standing by the door, and she smiled thinly.

'Goodnight, Simon!' She could hardly utter the words, but her face was impassive and she gave no indication of what she was feeling.

He departed, and she listened to his footsteps fading along the corridor. Then a bitter sigh escaped her and she felt tears prickling in her eyes. What would life be like with no Simon Morrell around? For a few moments she was filled with self pity, and then a frown touched her forehead and she shook her head slowly. If his fiancée was coming to St Catherine's then why was he intent upon leaving? It was a sudden decision! Something had happened this very day to make him arrive at it.

Suddenly Andrea could bear the suspense no longer, and she stood up quickly and left the office, walking along the corridor to the theatres. Nurse Speldon was still on duty, and the girl had read part of the letter Simon had received. Perhaps she could shed some light upon the apparent mystery.

Rita Speldon was sitting in the anteroom, stitching new tapes on the surgical gowns that had returned from the laundry. The girl looked up at Andrea's entrance, then looked down at her work quickly, and Andrea moistened her lips as she tried to think of the right words with which to open the conversation.

'Nurse, that business this morning!'

'Yes, Sister?' There was defiance in the girl's expression as she met Andrea's intent gaze.

'I haven't mentioned this to Mr Morrell, obviously. It is something we both want to forget. But Mr Morrell has been acting very strangely since he received that letter, and I'm wondering if it contained bad news of any kind.'

'I didn't get the chance to read all of it!' A thin smile touched the girl's lips and her blue eyes seemed to mock Andrea.

'Mr Morrell has told me that he made a difficult decision today. I can't tell you what it is, but I have the feeling that he is in some kind of trouble, and I was wondering if there was something we could do about it. What did you read in that letter?'

'If I tell you then it will be as sneaky of you in asking as it was for me to read it,' came the sharp reminder.

'I have a different reason for wanting to know,' Andrea reminded the girl. 'In any case, I was accused this morning of reading that letter. You were fortunate that I came into the locker room and caught you and not Mr Morrell himself. He knew he dropped the letter in the corridor, and he saw you there at the time.'

Nurse Speldon chuckled. 'So circumstances went against you! I'm sorry, Sister. But I like Mr Morrell, and I thought that coming into your team would give me the chance to make a play for him. I only wondered if he had a girl friend somewhere, and that's why I read the letter. It is from his ex-fiancée!'

'Ex-fiancée?' Andrea felt a weight begin to lift from her mind, and suddenly she saw light in the mystery. 'You said fiancée this morning. That's why I couldn't understand why he would suddenly decide to consider leaving here.'

'Is he going to leave?'

Andrea dragged herself from her thoughts, and she shook her head. 'I was thinking aloud then. Please forget what I said, Nurse. This mustn't get around the hospital, and there was nothing definite said, anyway. You said this ex-fiancée was coming here to work.'

'That's right. As you know there's a new theatre opening here very shortly and we're going to need another Sister and a whole new team. Mr Stevens is going to start heading his own team.'

'That's common knowledge,' Andrea said. She had been impatiently waiting for that day to dawn because it would mean that she wouldn't see so much of Clifford Stevens when he had his own surgical team.

'Well Cora Bayliss is coming to act as Theatre Sister to Clifford Stevens. It said so in the letter.'

'How did you know she is Mr Morrell's ex-fiancée?'

'It said in the letter that when she arrived she hoped they would be able to make it up.'

'Thank you, Nurse!' Andrea was breathing freely again. Hope was swelling in her heart once more, but she kept her face expressionless as she looked into her subordinate's pale blue eyes. 'Don't let any of this go any further, please.'

'The sooner I forget it the better,' came the sharp reply.

Andrea left the theatre and went back to her office, and she trembled on the brink of releasing her controlled emotions. There was still a chance that she could be successful in her quest for love with Simon. She had no idea what had caused the rift between him and his fiancée, but his decision to leave because she was coming here proved that he had not forgiven her anything. If he had fallen out of love with Cora Bayliss then he was free, and anyone who could interest him would be ethically at liberty to do so.

She sat down and went through her paperwork, her mind almost at ease now, and even her tiredness seemed to have evaporated. She looked round at the door when she heard footsteps in the corridor, and then a knock at the door made her hope that Simon had returned. But it was Clifford Stevens who entered, and he paused in the doorway, his face showing hopefulness as he gazed at her.

'I thought I'd find you here, knowing you are on stand-by,' he said. 'May I come in? Is that coffee I can smell?'

'It's getting cold now,' Andrea told him, 'But you're welcome to a cup. What are you still doing here?'

'There's a case that might have to come into surgery around midnight,' he said, entering and closing the door. He sat down in the seat Simon had used, and Andrea poured him a cup of coffee then resumed her seat. 'I know you always stick around until about ten when you're on first call. You're not too busy to talk, are you?'

'I'm always busy, but I've got through most of my paperwork. What's on your mind? You look worried about something.'

'I'm not worried.' He stirred the coffee and stared into the cup for some moments. 'But I do have something on my mind. I'm beginning to think in circles, and this is affecting my work. Did you hear how Morrell was tearing into me today?'

'Yes!' Andrea shook her head slowly as she considered the long day. 'But he had something on his mind too!'

'Oh! And what was that?'

'He didn't confide in me! But it was obvious to everyone. We all seem to have problems, but we ought to leave them out of the theatre!'

'That's easy to say, but if you get a real problem you can't shelve it at will. At least, I can't. I'm slowly getting worse and worse, and the Lord knows what will happen when I get into the new theatre with my own team.'

'You'll be handling the simple operations, that's all.'

'That's right, and I don't like it. I'd like to have you come with me as my theatre Sister, but you're too valuable on major ops. I'm going to get some stranger. But Morrell doesn't deserve you. He doesn't appreciate you.'

'He doesn't have to. I'm here to work, and that's what I do. But what's on your mind, Clifford? What's bothering you?'

She watched his lean face as he drank his coffee before answering. He was a tall, thin man with black hair and brown eyes, and he usually had a doleful expression on his face.

There wasn't much Andrea knew about him. He had been at the hospital for more than a year, and he had always worked on her team. He had been out with one or two of the nurses, but he didn't seem to be the type to get serious about a girl, although he was a serious type. He always seemed to have something on his mind.

'I'm in love with you, Andrea,' he said at length, watching her intently.

She caught her breath at his words, and her heart seemed to miss a beat. She firmed her lips and stared at him, unable to think of anything to say.

'That's what I thought,' he went on morosely. 'You're speechless! It's shocked you. But it tells me one thing. You don't have any feelings for me. I must have asked you a hundred times for a date, but you either haven't got the time or the inclination. But I'm in a bad state over you, and if I don't do something about it then I'm afraid something will snap.'

'I'm sorry!' She spoke hesitantly, searching for words. 'I think you're a very nice person, Clifford, but as you can see, I don't have any feelings for anyone. You've learned in the year that you've been here that I don't go around with anyone, and I'm not going to start it. I'm not the type, I suppose!'

'It wouldn't hurt you to go out with me once in a while,' he retorted.

'It would do a lot of harm,' she retorted. 'It

might give you ideas, and it would certainly strengthen any feelings you have.'

'You've got it all worked out, haven't you?' There was bitterness in his thin tones. 'There's no room in your life for anything but this place. You're dedicated! You're going to wind up like Sister Anstey, an old maid with nothing inside her but a programme of nursing routines. Or you'll turn into another Sister Cole!'

'I sympathise with your feelings for me, because I cannot requite them, Clifford. I'm afraid there's nothing I can do to help you. I'm certain that if you looked around you'd find some nice girl who would be only too pleased to go out with you, and if you became interested in someone else you'd soon forget me.'

'Don't talk to me as if I were a child,' he said sharply. 'This isn't an infatuation that I feel for you! I'm crazy about you. It's so bad that I can't sleep at night and my work is beginning to suffer. Something's got to be done before I blow my top.'

She stared at him, helpless for a moment, and she wondered why complications seemed to be piling up around her. She felt as if a great weight had been placed upon her shoulders, and when she took a deep breath she was almost stifled.

'Can't you find anything in your heart for me?' he demanded hopefully, getting to his feet and coming across to her desk. He stood

85

looking down at her, his dark eyes afire with emotion, and she saw his hands were trembling.

'I'm sorry, Clifford, but you're making things very difficult for the both of us. I'm not in love with you, and couldn't begin to feel anything even remotely resembling love. I don't know what to suggest to help you, but you'll have to pull yourself together and try to put this out of your mind.'

He shook his head almost angrily, and reached out his long, thin hands and took hold of her by the shoulders, lifting her easily from the chair. The next instant he was kissing her fervently, holding her in a grip which she could not break. He took her by surprise, and for some moments she could not resist, and then she began to struggle.

His mouth was pressed against hers, cutting off her breath, and Andrea knew a moment of panic as she failed to break his grip. The edge of the desk was pressing sharply against her thigh, and she almost lost her balance as he bore down upon her. She could hear the harsh sound of his breathing, and his arms were like steel bands around her.

When he momentarily lifted his face from hers to gasp for breath, Andrea spoke sharply to him, trying to bring him back to his senses, but he was past reason, and returned to her, holding her more powerfully than before.

Andrea used all her strength to try and push

him away, and she managed to twist away from the desk, where he had trapped her. She could not break his hold upon her, but began to lean away from him. She managed to move towards the door, and he went with her, holding her desperately, mouthing unintelligible phrases between the spates of kissing which he forced upon her.

Then he stepped on her foot, and Andrea, pulling backwards, lost her balance and fell heavily to the floor in front of Sister Cole's desk. Stevens couldn't save himself and came blundering down beside her, hurting her with his weight. Andrea lay still, breathless and shaken, and Stevens was gasping at her side.

At that precise moment, Andrea heard the office door open, and she looked up quickly, thinking that Nurse Speldon was coming in for fresh instruction, but to her horror she found Sister Cole staring down at her, and despite her shock, Andrea saw the malicious triumph that streaked into the sharp features of her superior.

CHAPTER SIX

There was tense silence while Andrea scrambled to her feet and faced Sister Cole, and Clifford Stevens was still breathless as he got up and stood with heaving shoulders, his composure gone and his emotions still rampant. Andrea could only stare into her superior's stiff face, and there was a sinking feeling in her breast as she waited for the trouble to start.

'I think you had better leave the office, Mr Stevens,' Sister Cole said stridently.

Stevens looked at Andrea, but she refused to meet his gaze. He swallowed noisily, then lurched towards the door, which Sister Cole opened quickly. When the door banged shut behind his departing figure, Sister Cole looked into Andrea's flushed face and waited in tense silence. Andrea met her superior's gaze unflinchingly, but she could think of nothing to say. She knew what she would have thought had she come upon such a scene that had met Sister Cole's eyes. But she knew she had to say something, and she took a deep breath and tried to compose herself. Her cap had come off and lay on the floor at Sister Cole's feet, and one of her cuffs was torn.

'Thank Heaven you came in when you did, Sister,' Andrea said. She went forward and picked up her cap.

'Don't try to pretend that Mr Stevens turned into a cave man!' came the sharp retort. 'I'm reporting this incident to Matron, and you can be ready to make an accounting to her about this. It's certainly out of my hands! I've never seen such disgraceful behaviour and there can be no excuses for it. You are on duty and so is Mr Stevens, and you know the rules of the hospital. I fully expect Matron to suspend you from duty, and you'll be extremely fortunate not to lose your job over this. But whatever happens, you'll certainly lose your position as my Assistant in this department. It could have been your duty nurse who came in! Think of the scandal if word of this went around the hospital.'

Andrea firmed her lips. She suppressed a sigh and turned back to her desk, knowing it would be useless trying to explain what had happened. It had looked bad, but she was being judged without the facts being taken into consideration, and she was aware that this was something that Sister Cole must have been praying for over the weeks.

Sister Cole kept on talking in the same harsh manner, but Andrea did not listen to her. She lifted the telephone and called the switchboard, reporting to the operator that she would be at home if needed for an emergency, and then she turned to leave the office.

'I've a good mind to suspend you from duty myself and take over,' Sister Cole said, barring her way to the door. 'I've never seen such disgraceful behaviour in all my days in a hospital. What an example to set younger nurses! You hold a position of great responsibility here and you haven't lived up to that level at any time while you've been a Sister. It's about time Matron knew of the situation that exists. Perhaps I'll be able to get a replacement while the team for the new theatre is being made up. I've had my fill of you, Sister!'

Andrea made an effort to remain silent. But she had to say something in her defence even though she knew Sister Cole would not listen.

'I know it's useless trying to explain to you, Sister,' she said slowly. 'But I was not responsible for what happened. It's most unfortunate that you walked in at that moment.'

'Most unfortunate, I agree,' came the terse reply. 'I don't know how long this sort of thing has been going on in this department while I'm off duty, but it's come to an end this evening. I don't want to hear your excuses, and it's no use trying to talk your way out of it. Save your explaining for Matron. I shall report this matter without fail.'

There was a smirk of triumph on her superior's face which sickened Andrea, and Sister Cole stepped aside and opened the door. Andrea departed silently, and the echoes of her footsteps in the tiled corridor seemed to hammer against the door of her heart.

Andrea was surprised to find the sun still shining as she left the hospital, and she paused at the gates for a moment, turning to look up at the many-windowed face of the great building, her thoughts sombre, her mind filled with despair. Why had Sister Cole chosen that

90

exact moment to return to the office? Why had Clifford Stevens lost control of himself in that way? The questions clamoured in her mind until she felt like screaming, and she turned slowly and walked to the bus stop. There were clouds in the sky and the sun was being blotted out. Angela suppressed a shiver although the evening was not cold.

A spot or two of rain began to fall, and she looked up at the sky, her thoughts distant. Her life had been singularly uneventful until Simon arrived at the hospital, she told herself. When she fell in love with him she invited trouble, and now she was hopelessly lost in her emotions and there seemed little hope of anything working out satisfactorily. She couldn't bring herself to blame Clifford Stevens for the way he had acted back there in the office. She knew how he must have felt. There had been times in the past when she had felt the impulse to throw herself into Simon's arms. But Sister Cole was going to make trouble. Of that there was no doubt. If anyone but her superior had walked into the office then it wouldn't have mattered so much.

When the bus arrived Andrea was standing in a steady downpour, and she smiled wryly because this particular stop didn't have a shelter. Her uniform was sopping wet as she boarded the bus, and the conductor made sympathetic clucking noises as he took her fare.

91

'I always thought nurses were like Girl Guides,' he said. 'You should always be prepared, Sister.'

She smiled, and some of her gloom dissipated as she looked from the window. She was a regular traveller on this route, and knew most of the conductors by sight. They all had a cheery word for her, and she appreciated this man's cheerfulness. But by the time they reached her stop the rain had eased, and she alighted thankfully and walked quickly home.

It was an effort to put on an act when she entered the house. Her parents were there, and Mrs Chaston asked the usual questions about Andrea's duty. Andrea escaped as quickly as she could, complaining of a headache, and she went up to her room and sat for a long time just wondering what to do about the situation which had arisen.

As far as the event which Sister Cole had witnessed was concerned, there was nothing she could do. It was completely out of her hands. Sister Cole would report it and Matron would have something to say. What might come of it Andrea had no way of knowing, but she didn't doubt that it would put her in a bad light in Matron's eyes. Sister Cole was certain to play up the whole thing. But it was more than Clifford Stevens and the problems he posed that worried Andrea. She was concerned about Simon. If he left St Catherine's then her life would suffer greatly.

She'd had some bad shocks during the day, and even now, knowing that Simon did not love Cora Bayliss, she was still unsettled by everything that had happened. She felt that if Simon had been fated to fall in love with her he would have realized it by now, or would at least have shown some signs of it.

Andrea was relieved when it was time to go to bed. She showered and wearily prepared to retire, and as soon as she had switched out the light and lay back to welcome sleep her brain began to whirl and she became wide awake.

For a long time she tossed and turned, sighing repeatedly as she failed to find rest. She could hear a heavy shower pattering down upon the garden, and slowly she began to sink down. Her mind began to relax and then she knew no more, until the sun peeping in at the window next morning brought her back to her senses . . .

Andrea opened her eyes and blinked, and found that her mind was labouring under a burden. She felt listless and washed out, as if she hadn't slept the whole night through. She knew she had slept badly, and she was still tired as she glanced at her watch and then hurriedly arose to start getting ready for the day. She was fifteen minutes late!

She skimped on breakfast and set out for the bus stop, arriving there just as the bus appeared around the corner, and there was a feeling of relief upon her as she boarded the vehicle. If she had missed it she would have been out of harmony for the rest of the day, and the day that lay before her was not pleasant to contemplate as it was.

When she arrived at the hospital she felt most reluctant to enter, but she steeled herself for the ordeal, and when she entered the corridor she almost walked into a man standing at the enquiry office. He stepped back from the window of the office as she reached him, and it was only her quick reflexes that saved her toes from being trodden. The man turned to apologize, and Andrea recognized him as Peter Barlow, who lived in the house next but one to her own.

'Peter! What are you doing here?' she demanded.

'Hello, Andrea!' He was tall and slim, darkly handsome, and she knew him as a sensitive, self-conscious young man. His father was dead, but had been a solicitor, and Andrea had known Peter since childhood. 'Mother was admitted yesterday.' His brown eyes were filled with uncertainty and despair.

'It's nothing serious, I hope!' Andrea was trying to recall the last time she had seen Mrs Barlow. She was certain her mother had not mentioned anything about their near-neighbour's health.

'She's been ill for a long time,' he said, shaking his head. 'Her doctor advised that she should come in here for examination, and

94

they've found cancer. She's being operated on today.'

'Oh, Peter, I am sorry!' Andrea put a hand on his arm, and her face was filled with genuine concern. 'What ward is she in? I'll go and have a chat with her.'

'Lady Mary Ward!' He glanced at his watch. 'I must hurry! I have been told that her operation is due this morning. I'll telephone later this afternoon.'

'I'm sure everything will be all right. Try not to worry.' Andrea knew the advice was useless in the circumstances, but there was little one could say to a person in Peter's situation. She saw him smile, and he turned to depart.

'Thank you, Andrea! You're in Theatre, aren't you? Will you be working on Mother's case?'

'I shan't know until I see the list in my office,' she replied. 'But you can be assured that everything possible will be done.'

'I know, but one cannot help worrying at a time like this. If your people have managed to catch it in time then Mother will be all right, but if it's too late then nothing will save her.'

He departed then, and Andrea stood staring after his tall, thin figure, her seemingly overwhelming troubles and problems quickly slipping into perspective in the face of his very real worries. She was thoughtful as she went on to the Department, and when she entered the office she found Sister Cole there as usual.

'Good morning, Sister!' Andrea had almost forgotten the trouble of the previous evening in the face of meeting Peter Barlow at the entrance. 'Is there a Mrs Barlow on our lists today?'

'Your list is on your desk, Sister!' came the sharp reply. 'I don't have a Mrs Barlow on my list. You can check yours yourself. I have a short list. I'm off duty this afternoon. But you'd better be ready to have an interview with Matron when it can be arranged.'

Andrea paused on the way to her desk and looked across at her superior, but she said nothing and took up her list. She didn't find Mrs Barlow's name on the list, and went back to Sister Cole's desk.

'Are you sure Mrs Barlow isn't on your list?' she demanded.

'Quite sure!' Sister Cole did not drop her gaze to the list before her.

'I understand that she was scheduled for an operation this morning.'

'And where did you get your information from? Surely I ought to be the first to learn of the fact in this department.'

'I've just been speaking to her son.' Andrea explained what had taken place. 'Someone told him the operation was to be performed today—this morning to be exact.'

'It may be another of those cases which they'll spring on us at the last minute.' Sister Cole sniffed deprecatingly. 'I'll make enquiries. Now I suggest you get along to your theatre and see that everything is ready for Mr Morrell to begin. I don't want to have to start checking your work after you've prepared. That's not the way the department should be run.'

Andrea glanced at her watch and saw that she had several minutes to spare before she had to go along to the theatre. She looked down at Sister Cole, but the older woman refused to meet her gaze.

'I would like to know just what is eating you, Sister,' she said firmly. 'Why is it that we can't get along without a lot of backbiting and friction? Is it me? I'm under the impression that my work is as near-perfect as possible. But if it isn't then I'm ready to be taught where I'm going wrong. I'm sure my manners and attitudes are compatible with yours. I don't hold strong opinions on anything. I don't countermand your orders or issue any of my own unless I check with you beforehand. But you've been down on me for a long time now, and I have the feeling it started when Nurse Harmer came into my team. Did she start carrying tales to you? Had you asked her to report on the way I handle my theatre? What is it that's biting you? Everyone around is beginning to notice, and the atmosphere is gradually deteriorating.'

Sister Cole raised her eyes to Andrea's face, and her features had slowly taken on a harsh tension that showed plainly just what she thought of Andrea's questions.

'Are you insinuating that I'm deliberately picking on you, Sister?' she demanded stridently. 'Because if you are you'll find that you won't get very far with Matron by making such accusations.'

'I'm not making insinuations or accusations,' Andrea said, tightening her lips. 'I'm making an effort to retrieve the situation here. These matters are slowly coming to a climax, and there will be trouble if something isn't done to stop the rot. I've been over this time and again in my mind, and I've even lost sleep over it. But I can find no valid reason for your behaviour. There's no reason why you should dislike me so much that you have to treat me like this.'

'If you think I'm harsh then it's because this department is getting lax in discipline. Look at the situation I walked into last evening! If that isn't indicative of what I mean then I'm no judge at all. Surely I don't have to put into plain words that I feel you are not the right person for the position which you occupy here!'

'I have the qualifications, and there have never been any complaints from the surgeons with whom I've worked. When I've stood in for you with Sir Humphrey I've been praised for the way I've done my work!'

'I'm not surprised that the surgeons are on

your side, Sister.' There was a grating note in Sister Cole's ragged voice. 'But looks aren't everything, although some of the male staff seem to think they are!'

'Is that it?' Andrea demanded tensely. 'Are you jealous of me, Sister? I can't help being attractive, and ten years younger than you!'

Sister Cole got to her feet with a quick motion, her face dark with anger.

'How dare you?' she demanded. 'If these are new tactics on your part to get at me then you're doomed to failure. I've sent a report to Matron about you, and if you're still working in this department after you've seen Matron about what happened last night then I shall be greatly surprised.'

Andrea looked into the woman's face, and saw something of the hatred showing in Sister Cole's dark eyes. She knew she would never get at the truth, and anything she said would only further inflame her superior. Sighing heavily, Andrea left the office and went to the theatre, and she was vibrating inside like an off-key tuning fork.

'Andrea, I must talk to you!' Clifford Stevens was standing in the doorway of the surgeon's room, and she paused and looked him in the eye.

'I should think you're satisfied with what you have done,' she retorted.

'I'm sorry!' He shook his head slowly, his face showing that he was deeply hurt. 'I'll go to

99

Matron and tell her exactly what happened last evening. I'll see to it that you're not in trouble for it.'

'That's big of you,' she said. 'But it shouldn't have happened in the first place. Now the damage has been done I suggest you stay out of it and let me patch it up as best I can.'

He nodded, his face showing despair, and Andrea went on to the theatre.

Simon was waiting for her just inside the theatre, and Andrea felt her heart seem to miss a beat at the sight of him. His face was serious and he could not keep his worry out of his impressive brown eyes. He sighed heavily when he saw her, and Andrea pushed all her anger and frustration into the back of her mind as she went towards him.

'What's wrong?' she asked softly, aware of Nurse Speldon in the background getting on with her duties. 'Is there anything you can tell me without giving away too much of your business? I can see that you've got something on your mind, Simon!'

He smiled gently. 'I'd like nothing better than to be able to cry on your shoulder,' he said. 'But it wouldn't help matters. I said last night that the only solution was to leave here, but after spending a near sleepless night I've come to the conclusion that I couldn't make a bigger mistake. I'm going to stay and face this out, and perhaps afterwards I'll be able to pick up some pieces and make something out of them.'

'You're talking in riddles as far as I'm concerned,' she told him. 'But if there is anything I can do to help you then you have only to say.'

'Do you mean that or are you only saying it to try and make me feel better?'

'I mean it!' She felt her nerves tighten, and there was a fluttering sensation in her breast. She longed to reach out and grasp his strong, skilled hands and tell him that she would willingly lay down her life for him, but she blinked and held herself in check. She was in enough trouble now because Clifford Stevens had been unable to control himself!

'Then there is something you could do for me.' He spoke slowly, as if reluctant to engage her services, and her heart quickened as she felt a surge of hope. 'We don't have time to talk now. Are you off duty this evening?'

'Yes. I shall be free when we've finished our list.'

'It'll be late. I have an unscheduled operation to perform, and I think we'd better do it first. It will put everything else back, but perhaps we can drop one or two minor cases off the list and do them tomorrow; as is always the case.'

'This unscheduled case! Is it Mrs Barlow?'

'Yes. Do you know her?'

'She lives a few doors from us. I saw her son at the hospital when I came in. Is it serious,

Simon?'

'I'm afraid it is!' He sighed heavily as he shook his head. 'If she had seen her doctor six months ago there might have been a chance for her, but I'm afraid all the tests show that her trouble is in an advanced stage, and I don't know what we're going to find when we open her up.'

Andrea nodded silently, and she was sad, her own worries paling into insignificance again. Then she drew a sharp breath.

'I'd better get ready, Simon. I'm in trouble as well. I shall be on the carpet before Matron as soon as there's time.'

'Really?' He frowned as he looked at her. 'What on earth have you been up to?'

'I'd rather not say, although I'd better hasten to add that it isn't anything I've done wrong. I've been compromised, I suppose, but I shall be in hot water because of it. Sister Cole will see to that. I tell you this so you won't be surprised if I get pushed out of here.'

'Pushed out! Is it as serious as all that!' Good Lord, Andrea, tell me about it. Is there anything I can do?'

She shook her head. 'I'll tell you about it later,' she retorted and moved away from him, going into the ante-room to scrub and prepare for theatre. When he had moved away from the doorway she glanced at the clock, and thought she had time to go to Lady Mary Ward to have a few words with Mrs Barlow. She telephoned the ward sister and learned that Mrs Barlow had not yet been given her pre-med, and Andrea went to Nurse Whittaker, explaining where she was going and asking the girl to do some of her work.

When she entered Lady Mary Ward, Andrea was met by the ward sister, who escorted her to Mrs Barlow's bedside. Andrea looked down at the woman's pale features, and faced the shocking situation with a cheery smile.

'Hello, Mrs Barlow!'

'Andrea! Andrea Chaston! I was wondering if I would see you in here!'

'I saw Peter this morning when I came on duty and he told me you were in here. How are you feeling, Mrs Barlow?'

'Not too good really, although I'd never tell Peter. The pain has got worse even in the short time I've been in here. But I'm not worried about myself. It's poor Peter I'm thinking of! What will become of him if anything happens to me?'

'You're going to be all right,' Andrea said. 'In fact you're coming down to me. I shall be with you right through the operation. We'll take care of you.'

'Thank you! I won't worry so much now. If you're going to be there then I know everything will be all right. If you see Peter, tell him I'm all right, won't you?'

'Of course! I'll make a point of seeing him,

Mrs Barlow. You don't have to worry about anything.' Andrea looked up as a ward nurse pulled the screens around the bed. It was time for Mrs Barlow's pre-med to be administered. She looked once more into the woman's dark eyes, noting the grey tinge in the features, and she patted the thin shoulder gently. 'I must go and get ready myself now, Mrs Barlow, and they're here to prepare you. I'll come and see you again after the operation.'

'Thank you for taking the time to come and talk to me,' the woman whispered, and her eyes filled with tears. 'It's made all the difference to me. I don't feel afraid any more.'

'I'll get Mother to come and visit you,' Andrea said. 'I'm sure she doesn't know you're in here, Mrs Barlow.'

The woman smiled and nodded, and the ward nurse approached with a syringe in a kidney dish. Andrea moved away from the bedside, paused for a moment to look at the sick woman, and then she turned and hurried out of the ward.

She was in the corridor leading to the theatres when a voice called to her, and when she turned quickly she found Matron coming towards her.

'Sister, I have received a disturbing report from Sister Cole. I'm sure you know all about it. When will you be able to come to my office to discuss it?'

'I'm due in theatre now, Matron, and it's

going to be a heavy day.'

'Very well! When you have time to spare perhaps you'll telephone my office and arrange with the Assistant Matron when it will be convenient for us to get together!' There was no expression in Matron's voice, but Andrea got the feeling that the axe was poised and ready to fall upon her unprotected neck. It didn't help her peace of mind as she continued towards the theatre.

CHAPTER SEVEN

When Andrea entered the theatre once more she found Simon there, talking with Clifford Stevens and the RSO. Andrea garbed herself, took a mask and gloves and put them on, and was ready. She hurried around doing her checks, and was satisfied that nothing had been overlooked. When her eyes strayed in Simon's direction she saw he was still talking intently to the two surgeons, and although his face was masked she was certain there was a frown upon it. Simon looked towards her and beckoned her and Andrea went obediently to his side.

'We'll have to remove the spleen,' Simon was saying when she moved into earshot. 'But that's not what I'm concerned about. I don't like the look of that shadow on the plates. I have the feeling there are going to be complications.'

'Is this Mrs Barlow's case?' Andrea asked, and Simon nodded.

'Yes. She'll be down shortly.'

'I have a list of the day's operations,' Andrea said. 'Do you want to make any changes now?'

'No, Sister, I think we'll push on as we have them listed, and this afternoon we can see how we are off for time. If we have to drop a couple of cases off the end of the list it won't matter so much. We can take them up tomorrow.'

'It's my day off tomorrow,' Andrea said. 'Sister Cole will be standing by.'

'I'm glad you told me.' Simon held her eyes for a moment, and Andrea was glad she was wearing a mask. His gaze was insistent, and she felt a trembling start deep within her.

'I'll just make one more check and then I shall be ready,' she said, hardly knowing what she was saying.

'The patient is coming up now,' Nurse Whittaker reported from the other side, and Andrea heard the sound of the lift and then the thud of the outer door of the anaesthetics room. She forced her mind to forget the forthcoming appointment with Matron and concentrated upon her duties. She moved her trolleys forward and glanced quickly around the theatre. There was mounting tension inside her as the patient was wheeled in and transferred to the operating table . . .

It was difficult for Andrea to forget that this patient was a woman she knew, and there was a picture of Peter Barlow's face in front of her eyes as the last minute preparations went ahead. The surgeons closed in on the table. David Hewitt was very busy with his machine, adjusting dials, checking, watching! The patient was shapeless under the sterile sheet, and Andrea forced away the last of her personal thoughts as she watched Simon apply the antiseptic paint to the area of operation.

She was ready with a scalpel when Simon held out his hand for it, and when he took it she offered up a silent prayer for this patient. The knife moved slowly and skilfully in Simon's gloved hand, opening the peritoneum at a stroke. Tension seemed to crowd them, closing in as the atmosphere grew heavy. She watched as Simon put his fingers into the cavity he had created, and his face turned slightly towards her as he explored the abdominal cavity. She could see that his eyes were narrowed, and although he seemed to be looking at her she knew he wasn't seeing her. In his mind's eye was the part of the anatomy upon which he was operating.

'We've got trouble,' Simon said suddenly, and a hiss of expelled breath sounded quickly from those around the table.

Andrea felt as if a giant hand squeezed her heart, and she firmed her lips behind her mask as she waited. She glanced towards David, seated on his stool at the patient's head, his gloved hands at work automatically, and he nodded slowly as he caught her eye. The silence seemed like a blanket, stifling them, and Andrea could hear the throbbing of a pulse in her temple.

'That shadow on the plate,' Stevens said in dry tones.

'That's it! I'll take out the spleen and then we'll see what we've got left.' There was no tremor in Simon's tones, and Andrea watched him intently, her mind thrusting up the knowledge she had of the spleen.

It was a strange organ high up under the edge of the rib cage, wedge-shaped and purplish, rarely as large as a man's fist when functioning normally. A number of blood diseases involved the spleen, which was connected closely with the white blood count, and it served as a graveyard for red blood corpuscles.

'How is she, David?' Simon's voice brought Andrea back from her thoughts.

'You can go ahead. Everything is under control at the moment.' David was scanning the dials, his blue eyes narrowed.

Simon continued, and if he was tense then his movements did not show it. There were beads of perspiration in his forehead, and from time to time his eyes lifted to meet Andrea's. The only sound in the theatre was the sibilant hiss of steam from the sterilizers.

Andrea held a small clamp ready. She knew what Simon had to do. And she could follow his progress by his movements although she could not see into the abdominal cavity. A second clamp was applied to the stalk of the spleen, and then Andrea put a scalpel into Simon's hand. He made a single, precise stroke between the clamps and the spleen came away easily.

Andrea had ligatures ready, and she was holding them out when Simon asked for them. He quickly secured the severed blood vessels, and then used a small, lighted spatula to look inside the cavity.

'I can see it,' he informed them in slow tones. 'There's a small stalk, and the growth is about the size of my thumb. I can see it quite clearly, but it's going to be difficult to get at. It's too deep to clamp, I think. I'll have to loop it and tie it off.'

Andrea was ready for him as he spoke, and she was holding out a long strand of suture fashioned with a tiny noose. Silence came as Simon endeavoured to lasso the extra organ by holding the noose over his opened fingers and inserting his hand into the cavity. He had to work blind, getting his fingers to move instinctively, and they all knew that if he made a mistake now and damaged the organ it could lead to a dangerous haemorrhage.

Tense moments passed as Simon made

several blind attempts to succeed, and each time he failed he had to withdraw his hand and get the noose set over his gloved fingers again. He had to secure the tiny stalk beyond the organ.

'How's the patient?' he demanded suddenly.

'All right so far,' David replied instantly. 'I'll warn you if there's any sudden change in her condition.'

'I've got it!' Simon paused, and Andrea heard his long, heavy sigh of relief. 'But I'd better put on a second one just in case.'

Andrea had already prepared a second, and it was ready when he held out his hand for it. Again they suffered the tension of passing moments, until finally Simon stepped back from the table for a moment and straightened his back. Andrea was holding a pair of long, curved scissors, and he took them from her and bent once more into his customary posture over the table. They all heard the gentle snip of the sharp blades as he severed the strange organ, and a moment later it lay in the palm of his gloved hand. Simon looked at it and then put it into the pathologist's tray, beside the spleen.

The clock on the wall seemed to be recording the passage of time twice as fast as usual, and Andrea caught the orderly's eye and nodded at him, signifying that it was time he went for his break. He gave her the thumbs up sign and departed silently, and Andrea

110

returned her attention to the operation.

She had prepared the sutures beforehand, and now passed them to Simon, who was stitching the abdominal lining. Relief was beginning to grow inside her. The operation looked like being a success. She was mentally crossing her fingers when David uttered something which was unintelligible but attracted all attention.

'What is it?' Simon demanded instantly.

'The pulse rate is dropping!'

Perspiration seemed to suddenly spring from Simon's forehead as he paused in his work, and he looked towards the anaesthetist. A nurse wiped his forehead and he lifted his shoulders with a deep breath. Andrea was stiff, filled with a sudden premonition, and she could feel a coldness swelling inside her, moving like a miniature glacier. She shivered as if Death itself had breathed icily upon the back of her neck. David was suddenly galvanized into action, and the sight of him working hurriedly made her fear the worst, for she knew he was not a man to panic. He was unflappable, but suddenly he was fighting for the patient's life.

Hewitt twirled a knob and there was the sudden hiss of oxygen, which was almost immediately cut off as a valve was closed.

'There's no heartbeat!' David said thinly.

Andrea was already holding a scalpel, and she slapped it into Simon's outstretched hand.

She had a picture of Peter Barlow before her eyes as she watched Simon make an incision in the wall of the patient's chest and insert his hand to begin massaging the still heart. Sweat was breaking out profusely on Simon's forehead, and Andrea could hear his ragged breathing behind the stifling mask as he worked relentlessly.

Nurse Whittaker was frozen in an unconscious pose by the sterilizers, her eyes bright as she stared at them grouped around the table. Nurse Speldon came forward to top up Andrea's saline bowl, and Andrea could hear the girl's harsh breathing. Tension held them and time seemed to stand still.

'There's no response,' David said in steady tones. He was sweating now, and his pale eyes were narrowed.

Simon made no reply. Andrea was praying subconsciously, her gloved hands clenched. Death had come among them, slipping into their company with intangible swiftness, their greatest enemy in the theatre, their constant reminder of reality.

The sweep second hand on the clock seemed to be moving much faster than normal. Andrea glanced at it with widening eyes. Her throat constricted. She was no stranger to death, but she didn't want to lose this patient. She watched Simon administer an injection, and still the seconds slipped by, taking with them the patient's waning chances of survival.

They all knew that after three minutes of death certain unalterable changes took place in the body which made recovery impossible. They were rapidly approaching the critical time, and Simon was getting no response at all.

'You're wasting your time now,' David said finally, and he was not being callous, Andrea knew.

Simon nodded and ceased working immediately, and he didn't look at Andrea as he backed slowly away from the table. She watched him turn and walk swiftly into the anteroom, and it was Clifford Stevens who finished off the work on the body.

'We'd better start getting ready for the next case,' David said softly, getting up from his stool. He was removing the tubes which connected his instruments to the patient, and his words broke the tension that held them.

Andrea nodded and sighed deeply, and she pointed at the door. Nurse Whittaker nodded and went to call the porters, who entered and removed the body. During the next fifteen minutes Andrea worked in a haze. She couldn't keep her personal thoughts out of her mind. When she thought of how she had visited Mrs Barlow, and could still hear the woman's last words in her mind, she couldn't really believe that death had stepped in. Poor Peter Barlow! There had been so much hope in his face as he'd departed. Now a policeman would be sent to contact him and he would learn the worst.

The rest of the morning went on and they performed two other operations, both successfully. When they stopped for lunch, Simon took hold of Andrea's arm as they walked across the theatre to the anteroom.

'I'm sorry about Mrs Barlow,' he said gently, pulling down his mask. His face showed strain and worry, and Andrea took a deep breath as she removed her mask. She gasped heavily for air for a moment then nodded.

'You didn't give her much chance before the operation, did you?' she demanded.

'She had stomach cancer which tests proved was inoperable,' he said slowly. 'The operation this morning was to make her more comfortable while she lasted. She didn't have much time in any case. It's one of those tragedies we're always coming up against. If she had seen her doctor six months earlier she would have had a better chance.'

Andrea nodded dully. She felt heavy-minded, and her head was aching intolerably.

'Shall I get the nurses back to start at two?' she demanded.

Simon nodded after glancing at the clock. 'Yes. We'd better push on while we can. There's still a lot to do, and I want to get done early so I can talk to you. May I drive you home after we get through here?'

'Thanks!' She nodded. 'I'll look forward to that.'

He smiled and patted her shoulder and went off, and Andrea turned to help with the cleaning up. Nurse Whittaker was already mopping the floor, and Nurse Speldon, who had paused to watch Andrea with Simon, went back to putting the general set into the sterilizer.

'We'll start again at two,' Andrea said. 'Get away as soon as you can.'

Both nurses nodded and carried on. Andrea bustled around, trying to lose her personal thoughts, but she was still heavy in spirit when she followed the nurses out of the theatre. She went into her office before going on to lunch, and saw Sister Cole at her desk. It crossed her mind that her superior was spending more and more time in the department these days! She looked into Sister Cole's face, and didn't like the smirk on the older woman's face.

'I presume you've seen Matron this morning,' Sister Cole said, cutting short Andrea's greeting.

'She asked me to make arrangements to see her! It won't be today, Sister.'

'So long as you get along to see her in the near future.'

'It's my day off tomorrow. I'll come in and see her in the morning.' Andrea's eyes were hard as she looked at Sister Cole. It was in her to take up the verbal war where they had dropped it the previous day, but she didn't feel equal to it, and turned away.

'You lost a patient this morning!' The tones suggested that Andrea was personally to blame for it.

'Yes. It was Mrs Barlow! She lived in my road. I knew her quite well!' Andrea sighed heavily.

'It was her son you were talking to when you came into the hospital this morning.'

'That's right.'

'Is he another friend of yours?'

Andrea didn't like the Sister's tones, but she said nothing. She left the office without replying, and her thoughts were mixed as she went to lunch. She was beginning to feel that this situation could not be tolerated much longer, and she smiled thinly when she thought that after she'd seen Matron the matter might well be out of her hands and changed for the worse.

The afternoon's work was routine, and although time seemed to drag, they reached the last case and handled it. Andrea was almost dropping from exhaustion as she finished putting the theatre to rights, and she dismissed the nurses and went along to the office. There was some paperwork to be done before she could finish, and she knew Simon would be coming for her as soon as he was ready.

She had hardly sat down at the desk, congratulating herself the while because Sister Cole was not present, when there was a knock at the door, and when she called out an invitation to enter she was surprised to see Peter Barlow standing on the threshold. His face was pale, plainly showing shock, and his dark eyes were slightly glazed and staring.

'Peter!' She got to her feet immediately and went to his side.

'Forgive me for coming here like this,' he said awkwardly. 'But I've been walking around in a daze ever since I got the news this morning. I can't really believe it. She was talking to me last night, and they said it wasn't going to be too serious. What happened to her, Andrea?'

'I am dreadfully sorry, Peter! I was there in Theatre when it happened. Everything possible was done to save her.'

He nodded slowly. 'I'm sure it was. But the shock of it has hit me hard. I can't believe it. I daren't go home. That empty house with all her things in it! What am I going to do, Andrea?'

She heard footsteps in the corridor then, and a sigh escaped her as she pulled forward a chair. 'Sit down for a moment, Peter,' she told him. 'Would you like a cup of coffee?'

'No thanks!' He looked around at the door when there was a knock, and he got to his feet. 'You're still busy. I shouldn't be here taking up your valuable time.'

'It's all right. Sit still, Peter.' She went to the door, but it opened as she reached out for the handle, and she found herself face to face with Simon.

'Ready to go home yet?' he demanded.

'I was just getting through some of the paperwork,' she replied. She let him see Peter Barlow, and then introduced the two men.

'I'm sorry,' Simon said, when he learned Peter's identity. 'I did everything that was possible.'

Andrea pictured again the grim scene in Theatre that morning, and she knew he had done all that he could. She caught Simon's eye, and shook her head slowly when she saw the query in his gaze.

'We're going home now, Peter,' she said. 'Can we drop you off? You ought to go home now, you know.'

'I think I'll walk for a bit longer,' he said. 'I'm sorry I bothered you, Andrea.'

'It's no bother.' She shook her head. 'We're old friends, Peter, and if there's anything I can do to help you then just say. You can't go wandering around like this. Have you eaten at all today?'

He shook his head miserably.

'We're going out to eat now. We've just finished for the day,' Simon put in. 'Would you come along with us?'

'Thanks, but I've taken up enough of your time as it is, and I'd rather be alone. Don't worry about me. It's helped just to have a few words with you, Andrea.'

She nodded, knowing there was nothing she could say to help ease the shock he was feeling. He got to his feet again and went to the door, departing without a word, and Andrea stood looking into Simon's face as they listened to his receding footsteps.

'Poor Peter! He's such a quiet, sensitive man. I've known him ever since we started school together, Simon. He's all alone now. I do hope he'll make out.'

'Poor chap! I only wish I could have saved his mother! But what can I say? We do the very best we can, and although it sometimes seems that we have a hand in saving life, the decision doesn't really rest with us. There's always a greater judgement than mine to be considered.'

Andrea nodded, knowing what he meant. She suppressed a sigh as she went back to her desk and sat down. She called the assistant matron's office and made arrangements to return to the hospital in the morning to see Matron. When she replaced the receiver she found Simon looking at her intently.

'What's wrong?' she asked.

'You're on the carpet for something and I'd like to know what it is.'

'I'd rather not say. If Matron takes no action then no harm is done, but if she does something about it then I suppose it will come out, and you'll learn of it soon enough.'

'That sounds bad. Is it something Sister

Cole has got you for?'

'She is involved, but it isn't trouble of her making. I can see that she's not being over zealous in making a report to Matron, but she ought to have found out the facts before she plunged in. I couldn't expect her to, anyway. She's had her knife into me for a long time now.'

'That's something I don't understand. I should imagine everyone can get along quite easily with you. What is wrong with Sister Cole?'

'I wish I knew. I went as far as to ask her last evening, but it didn't help.'

'Let me know if there's anything I can do to help,' he said. 'Shall we leave now?'

Andrea nodded and got to her feet and they left the hospital. When they were seated in Simon's car she looked at him, tingling a little at their nearness.

'There was something you wanted to ask me,' she said. 'Perhaps you'd better attend to that before driving me home.'

'You think I might not be able to keep my mind on my driving?' He smiled thinly. 'I think I've changed my mind about enlisting your help. It sounded like a good idea when I put it to myself. But after asking you to help I've come to the conclusion that it won't be any use. I've already decided that I won't leave here. I was going to, you know.'

'So you said.' Andrea's face bore a frown as

120

she looked into his dark eyes. She recalled the anguish she had felt at his decision, and she couldn't help feeling that the situation might still turn against her. But he seemed set upon staying now, and if he had no love for his ex-fiancée then there was little to worry about the girl getting back to him. But that must be what she was trying to do. If she had deliberately sought him out then there could be only one reason why. She wanted him back.

For a moment Andrea was tempted to tax him about the situation, but then she realized that she was not supposed to know anything at all about Cora Bayliss. She tried to curb her impatience as he started the car and drove out of the park.

'Shall we go somewhere to eat or do you want to go home?' he demanded.

'I ought to change out of uniform, but you can have something to eat at my home. My parents have gone out for the evening. I can get you something to eat.'

'I wouldn't want to put you to any trouble.' He shook his head. 'You're as tired as I am. Someone should be around to get you what you need.'

'I'm not about ready to fall down from sheer exhaustion,' she retorted with a smile. 'But I'm next door to it.'

He chuckled, and for a moment his brown eyes were clear of the shadows that had filled them all day. Andrea watched him as he drove out of the park and into the stream of traffic. They were fairly untalkative during the drive through town, and she found it difficult not to lean back and close her eyes. She knew that if she did she would be asleep in next to no time, and that was the last thing she remembered. Her head lolled to one side and her eyelids fluttered. The jolting of the car lulled her and she didn't remember dozing off.

What brought her awake, however, was the pressure that came suddenly on her mouth. She opened her eyes with returning awareness and thought she was still asleep and dreaming, for Simon was kissing her very gently on the lips!

CHAPTER EIGHT

Simon drew away from her, a tight little smile on his lips, but his eyes were narrowed and calculating as he held her startled gaze. She could only stare at him, her mouth tingling strangely from the impact he had made.

'That's better,' he said softly. 'You were asleep, and it seemed the best way to wake you.'

'You kissed me!' she said, and she could imagine that her eyes were wide with astonishment.

'So?' He was watching her closely, his head

held on one side. 'You shouldn't fall asleep in a strange man's car.'

'You're not a strange man,' she retorted. 'And I remember telling myself when we left the hospital that I mustn't close my eyes. But you kissed me!'

'All right!' He sighed. 'I'll confess to the greatest crime of the century. I kissed you. I've got no defence. All I can say is that I don't know what came over me. When I stopped the car I saw you were asleep. Something seemed to give inside me. You looked so peaceful and attractive, so defenceless, that I couldn't resist making contact with you.'

'Are you that lonely deep inside?' she questioned.

He chuckled and opened his door, getting out of the car to walk around to her side, and Andrea looked out of the window to see that they had arrived at the house. She felt weak at the knees as she alighted from the car, and he took her elbow as she swayed. But she felt as if she were walking on air as they went into the house. Her lips were tingling from the kiss, and she wished she had been awake at the time. There was a raging turmoil deep inside her, and she was once again experiencing the strange impulse to throw herself into his arms.

'Come into the kitchen,' she said. 'I'll get us something to eat.'

'I really ought to go. I've got some work to do.'

She caught her breath as she met his gaze, and something inside her protested at his words.

'Oh no!' She couldn't prevent her cry. 'Don't go yet.'

He looked into her eyes, and she was aware that they were standing very close together in the hall. She heard his sharp intake of breath, and a muscle twitched in his cheek.

'Something seems to tell me that I ought to go, and never see you again outside of the hospital,' he said slowly in jerky tones.

'That sounds strange!' She was breathless, with a tight feeling in her heart that threatened to stifle her. 'What's wrong with me?'

'There's nothing wrong with you! Heaven knows there's too much right with you.' He reached out a trembling hand and let the tips of his long fingers touch her cheek. 'What kind of a girl are you, Andrea? I've worked with you for three months and I still don't know much about you. During the past twenty-four hours I've learned a little, but not as much as I'd like. You're one of the most beautiful girls I've ever met, and yet you don't appear to have any romance in your soul. You're a dedicated nurse! That's what you are! You can't see anything beyond your duty at the hospital!'

'Is that wrong then?' she asked unsteadily.

'Of course it's wrong, when you're playing havoc with the feelings of the people who work with you!' He moistened his lips, and she saw

124

him shake his head slowly. 'Look,' he went on earnestly, and his voice was pitched much lower. 'I'm talking out of turn. If I had run my life differently before I came to St Catherine's then perhaps I would have some right to talk in this fashion, but I can't start anything that might lead to trouble, although I don't know how I can stop myself doing something.'

'You've lost me somewhere,' she told him.

'I'm not surprised.' He smiled ruefully. 'You're a wonderful girl, Andrea. I've never met anyone quite like you before. But I'm afraid a beautiful dream must be crushed before it engulfs us. I'm being a fool! I ought to keep my mouth shut and turn around and get out of here.'

'What reason could you have for not being friendly with me?' She watched him closely, wondering exactly what lay in his past. She was thinking of what Rita Speldon had told her, but the part-contents of one half-read letter couldn't reveal the whole situation which he had left behind at his previous hospital.

'That's the whole trouble!' He shook his head almost angrily. 'What possible reason could there be to keep me away from you? I've seen the expression in your eyes sometimes when you've looked at me, Andrea! I've speculated upon it a great many times, and I've had to fight every natural instinct I possess to keep away from you.'

She listened to his words with growing

amazement. In her most intimate dreams she had always pictured him as being secretly in love with her, and she had ached to hear him tell her so. Now he was practically admitting it, and yet there was some deep reason why he should not act naturally towards her.

He suddenly put his hands upon her shoulders, and Andrea felt her knees weaken. She caught her breath, holding herself stiff as she tried to fight her love. It seemed to her that she had always been in love with him, and he had been remote, unattainable. She could hardly accept the events of the past day. Now all the barriers between them were down and it seemed that he had a great deal of feeling for her.

'Andrea!' His voice was overloaded with emotion, and suddenly he was nervous and excited and she was breathing harshly as she tried to hold her impulses in check. But they drew close together as if one were a magnet and the other a piece of inanimate metal. How she finished up in his arms Andrea never afterwards knew, but she was there suddenly, in his embrace, feeling the strength of his arms about her and clutching at him as if her life depended upon their being together.

She closed her eyes as she felt his warm breath on her cheek, and the whole world seemed to tilt and revolve. The rush of emotion which struck through her almost took her senses, and she might have fallen but for his strong arms. Her thoughts seemed to die in her mind. There was only one sensation in the whole world. His mouth came slowly against hers, awakening such desires in her that she was surprised by their existence. She let go her tight hold upon reality and drifted seemingly on a magic carpet into the realms of ecstasy.

It seemed like an eternity that they were locked in embrace. Time had no meaning for either of them. In the back of Andrea's mind a pulse seemed to beat out a crazy message. She felt her inner defences crumble like the walls of an age-old castle falling to decay. The stiffness of her normal manner fled before the hot, resounding thrills of contact with this man she had loved desperately for weeks.

When they eased apart, Andrea could not stand, and Simon kept a strong arm about her waist. His face was very serious as he looked at her.

'That was the last thing that should have happened,' he said quietly. 'We've taken that last irretrievable step, Andrea. I sensed that you had fallen in love with me, but I couldn't accept it. Every time I looked at you I couldn't help seeing your dedication to your work. I told myself it was just my foolish wishful thinking that made me believe that you could love me. I've been trying to tear my emotions apart for weeks now, fighting against falling for you. But each day brought me deeper into the situation we've got before us. I'm in love with you, Andrea, and it hurts.'

She couldn't speak. Her throat was constricted and her mind was blank. Her only awareness was of requited love, and a fierce elation filled her, made her let her ordinary reserve melt away as snow disappears in a thaw.

'I've been in love with you from the first moment I met you,' she admitted in low tones. 'I've been tearing my mind to pieces over you, Simon.'

'I guessed it, and there was nothing I could do to help you. I didn't have the right to stop you, and when I found myself being attracted to you I couldn't help hoping that perhaps this was what Fate had in store for us. But I don't think it can be, Andrea. In fact I know that we'll never be able to go beyond this stage.'

'How can that be? Now that we both know what the other feels! What could stand in our way?' The words were torn from her heart. She looked into his face with such agony showing in her eyes that he reached out and touched her cheek tenderly.

'Poor Andrea! Have you ever been in love before?'

'Never!' She shook her head impatiently.

'Then how do you know this is love?'

'Every girl knows love when it comes. But what's wrong in your life, Simon? Are you here in Surlington because you're running away from something?'

'You might put it like that, but it hasn't done any good. My past is catching up with me.'

'Cora Bayliss!' The name escaped Andrea's lips, and she saw Simon start in surprise.

'So you did read my letter!' His dark eyes were filled with an undefinable expression, and she shook her head quickly.

'No. It isn't what you think.' She explained what had happened, and saw him nod.

'Well I didn't think I would be able to keep it all a secret,' he admitted earnestly. 'I suppose it was bound to come out.'

'Let me get us something to eat,' she interrupted softly. 'If you feel like telling me about it then come into the kitchen while I'm busy.'

He nodded slowly. 'I owe you an explanation, I guess. Andrea, if you only knew my feelings!'

'If they're anything like mine then you have my sympathy,' she retorted.

'I've almost been driven insane during the evenings when I've known you were off duty. I've come past this house a great many times in my car, hoping just for a glimpse of you. I've walked around the town hoping to bump into you, but Fate was never kind enough for that to happen. But now here I am, here in your home with you, and I've learned that you love me.'

'And you love me!' She said the words as a challenge, wondering if he would deny the fact, and she saw him smile slowly and shake his head wonderingly.

'I do love you! Surely no man in his right senses could look at you and not feel something. Those beautiful eyes of yours! The times they peered at me over your mask! Heaven knows how I managed to keep my mind on what I was doing in Theatre. It was most disconcerting to be in love with you, trying to conceal it when we were together so often.'

He paused in the kitchen doorway and took hold of her with a quick eagerness. But he didn't kiss her. He held her close and kept his arms tightly around her. She could hear his shuddering breath, feel a trembling in him, and she closed her eyes and uttered a silent prayer of thanks to the fates that had permitted this.

'You've been unhappy in the past, haven't you?' she asked, disengaging herself from his embrace and leading the way into the kitchen.

'That's hardly the word for it,' he admitted, sitting down at the table. 'Let me tell you about it while I have the opportunity. If it gets around the hospital you may hear a garbled account, and while I don't care what the others may think, you're the only one I want to know what really happened.'

Andrea busied herself preparing a meal, thankful that the maid had gone out. But she listened to Simon's intense voice while he talked, and her mind avidly took in his words.

'Cora Bayliss!' He said the name as if it were poison on his lips. 'She's a theatre Sister, Andrea, but not a patch on you. I was a fool to fall for her winsome ways. Her father was senior surgeon at the hospital where I worked, and I suppose that has been the main stumbling block, the keystone to her assault on my life.' He smiled thinly at her as she turned to look at him. 'Does that sound too dramatic?' he demanded. 'Perhaps I've made the mistake of thinking that it all meant much more than it was in reality. But a patient died and that is the ultimate in a surgeon's life.'

'You were responsible for a patient's death?' There was a quiver in Andrea's voice as she asked the question.

'Indirectly! It was the evening when Cora and I became engaged. I had a patient under observation, and I knew it was a critical time. If we had to go into surgery then it would be urgent. Of course I followed the usual routine of letting the hospital know my whereabouts for the evening, and the message arrived at Cora's house. She took it and kept it from me because she thought my absence from the party would spoil her evening. Can you believe that a professional nurse would do such a thing?' There was bitterness in his tones, and he shook his head as if he still couldn't believe what had happened.

'She made an error of judgement!' Andrea

said generously.

'If it had been the only incident I might have agreed, but you don't know Cora! She hooked on to me and I was flattered, I suppose. I fell for her, or at least I thought I did. But I soon became disillusioned, and then I found that I couldn't get free of her. She made my life a complete hell. It ended when I came here. But you know now that she's found me, and she's coming here to work. That's why I said I'd leave, Andrea, but when I came to make the decision I found that you meant too much to me. I can't go. I've got to stay because of you, and when Cora does arrive and she finds out that I love you there's going to be trouble.'

'Is that all you're worried about?' Andrea demanded.

'You're making the mistake that I made in the first place,' he retorted. 'You're under-estimating Cora!'

'Or you're underestimating the power of love,' Andrea countered swiftly.

He watched her movements for a moment, his eyes filled with wonder, and then he buried his chin in one hand and put his elbow on the table. His dark eyes burned as they stared at her.

'I wonder if you have something there!

'I'm sure I have!' Her heart was thudding swiftly as she faced him. 'I know you can't put the bad things of your life behind you, but if this woman is your only worry now then I advise you to forget about her. She may have had some power over you at your other hospital, but here she'll be just another Sister, and I doubt if there's anything she can do to make my life any worse.'

'Sister Cole has been giving you a bad time, hasn't she?' He sighed. 'We all seem to have our problems.'

'And we survive them. That's the main thing to remember, Simon.' Her tones carried confidence, and she saw his eyes clear as he felt the power of her determination.

'I'm willing to give it a try.' He smiled grimly. 'What have I got to lose?' Then he nodded, and his face hardened. 'But I have everything to gain. I'll tell you what I planned to ask you to do for me, shall I?'

'I'm curious to know! I wouldn't be a normal woman if I didn't feel an urge to know.'

'When I told you today that I wanted to see you this evening to ask you a favour I had some crazy idea in the back of my mind that if Cora came here and found that I had fallen for someone else she would have to forget her own plans for me.'

'You want us to pretend that we're in love?'

'Or just walking out together!' he said hopefully.

'But if she starts asking around the hospital she'll soon find out that we haven't been together long.'

133

'Don't try to find obstructions to the idea. Let's be constructive about it. The fact that I am seeing someone else, regardless of the duration of our friendship, should be sufficient to put a crimp in Cora's designs. That's all I ask.'

'All right. I'll go along with it,' Andrea said promptly.

'But I'm not asking you to do that now,' he retorted.

'But I think it's a good idea, and it might just work.'

'All right.' He was smiling now. 'So let's give it a try. I have been trying to get to know you for weeks, and this way is as good as any. But be warned, Andrea. When Cora gets here and learns that we are together she's going to try and make a lot of trouble for you.'

'I'll take my chances on that,' Andrea retorted.

They spent the rest of the evening together, and Andrea was delighted with the way events were shaping. By the time Simon decided to go his way home they were through talking about possibilities and probabilities, and there existed between them a tacit understanding of the fact that they were drawn to one another and wanted to progress naturally towards a closer basis of friendship.

When they stood at the door, Andrea suddenly recalled that she had to see Matron next morning, and when she mentioned the fact Simon put a hand on her arm.

'I've been so excited about this evening that I completely forgot to ask you what you're going to do with yourself tomorrow, after you've seen Matron.'

'I hadn't decided to do anything in particular. I expect to get some trouble in the morning, and that will probably ruin my day.' She smiled grimly, shaking her head as she looked into his shadowed face.

'Well I've wangled tomorrow off as well, and I meant to ask you earlier if you'd care to spend some time with me.'

'I'd love to!' Andrea replied without hesitation. 'I have to be at the hospital at ten. I suppose Matron will get through with me within half an hour.'

'All right. I'll be in the hospital car park around ten-thirty, waiting for you. If we're going around together the sooner we let people see us in public the better.'

'I'll be looking for you,' she promised.

His face turned more serious then, and Andrea tensed for a moment. She fancied he was going off without kissing her goodnight, but he took her gently into his arms and held her close. When he kissed her, Andrea was filled with delight, and she held tightly to him, afraid to let him go in case her dreams went with him. It seemed too great a miracle to be believed! After all the weeks of hoping and waiting and wondering, the seemingly

135

impossible had come to pass.

Simon finally departed, and Andrea went to bed. She was tired, but an inner excitement kept her mind vibrant with conjecture. She realized that there were some difficulties facing them, but all love found sticky patches, and difficulties were merely measuring sticks with which to test the degree of their love. She slept with an easy mind, but when she awoke in the morning she found herself filled with anticipation and nervousness.

Precisely at ten, Andrea presented herself to the Assistant Matron, and Mrs Rayner tried to set her mind at ease. But Andrea was past being comforted, and when she was shown into the presence of Matron she felt like a schoolgirl summoned before the head for some obscure misdemeanour.

'I appreciate that this is your day off, Sister,' Matron said, regarding Andrea critically through her tinted glasses. 'But you are no doubt aware of the seriousness of the report which has come to me.'

'Yes, Matron!' Andrea felt her nervousness dissipate now she was actually facing her superior.

'Pull up a chair and sit down, please.'

Andrea was faintly surprised by the instruction, but she obeyed, and sat by a corner of the desk. Matron regarded her for some moments, and what seemed to Andrea like an awkward silence began to make itself apparent, but Matron sighed heavily and shook her head.

'From what I know of you, Sister, I would say that you have a good explanation for what Sister Cole saw in your office. I don't know if I want to hear it. Sister Cole did the right thing in making a report about it, but I have been hearing some disturbing reports about the situation in your department. However since a report of this somewhat embarrassing incident has been made I must check it to a logical conclusion. I won't read Sister Cole's report, but I hope you can explain what happened to my satisfaction. I don't have to tell you how strict we have to be in this sort of thing. It might well have been one of your subordinates who walked into the office at that precise moment.'

'Matron, I can hardly explain what happened without making an accusation.' Andrea shook her head. 'As I was on duty I will assume full responsibility for the incident.'

'That's good enough for the report, but not good enough for me, Sister. Ordinarily if a nurse was brought before me on a similar charge I would either suspend her from duty until a full investigation was made or she would be dismissed.'

'What happened was not with my consent or co-operation, Matron,' Andrea said tensely. 'I was taken by surprise, and it was during the struggle to get away that I slipped and fell to the floor.'

'I see. You make no mention of Mr Stevens, although Sister Cole does in her report. Has this sort of thing ever happened before between you and Mr Stevens?'

'No, Matron. Mr Stevens asked me several times to go out with him. I always refused. Last night he came into the office while I was doing my paperwork. He told me he's in love with me, and asked me if there was any hope for him. When I told him there wasn't he just grabbed me. There was nothing I could do about it. It was unfortunate that Sister Cole entered the office at that time.'

'I agree with you, Sister.' Matron sighed as she glanced down at the papers before her on the desk. 'Sister Cole has always been a stickler for discipline, which is a good thing unless the habit is carried to excess. I've heard some of the stories going around the hospital. I understand from other quarters that you and Sister Cole are not getting along together.'

'I'm not going to tell tales, Matron, but there is a change in Sister Cole's manner. It was gradual at first, but now the situation is becoming intolerable. I have been considering coming to see you to discuss it, but I've been afraid that if anything were said to Sister Cole she would think I had gone over her head.'

'Are you the main butt for her displeasure?'

'I think so, but everyone is getting trouble from her.'

'Have you any idea why she's taken on this attitude?'

'None at all. I've racked my brains, but I just can't find any reason. I've always done my duty perfectly. You must know that I am not satisfied with anything less than my best.'

Matron remained silent for a moment, considering, and the silence seemed to take Andrea by the throat. Then her superior was looking at her with piercing gaze.

'Sister, I've already decided to take no action on this incident which Sister Cole reported. As a matter of fact I had a word with Sir Humphrey as soon as I learned of this, and he questioned Mr Stevens about it. It is clearly obvious that you are not to blame in this so we can forget the matter. But I asked you to come in to see me because I want to go into this business of the situation that exists in your department. There are some changes to be made in the future, and we must of course look ahead. The new wing is going to be built in due course, although that is still some way ahead. But the new Theatre will soon be ready for operation, and I'm already getting staff together for it. There is a Sister coming to take over, and I have to promote one of the nurses in the department. I have spoken to Sister Cole about this, and although I won't name her choice for promotion, I want to know what you think about the nurses. You are Sister Cole's assistant, and you ought to be in a position to pass judgement.'

'Well I don't have to think about that at all, Matron,' Andrea said instantly. 'Nurse Whittaker is the most able person in the department.'

'That's my idea of the most likely candidate,' Matron agreed. 'I've had some disturbing reports about Nurse Harmer!'

Andrea frowned. Surely Sister Cole hadn't put forward Nurse Harmer's name for promotion! No matter what her faults were, Sister Cole had always put duty first, and the good of the hospital was her only consideration. But this! She shook her head, and then became aware that Matron was watching her.

'I can tell by your face what you think of Nurse Harmer as a candidate,' the older woman said. 'I have had reports on her work, of course, and I know that Mr Morrell refuses to have Nurse Harmer in the same Theatre.'

'If Sister Cole did put up Nurse Harmer's name then I can only say that there's something wrong with her judgement. I'm in no position to speak out against my superior, but I do think you should investigate this Matron. Perhaps Sister Cole is ill! She certainly hasn't been acting normally.'

'But you are in a position to speak out. You're second in command in the department, Sister, and it is your duty to see that everything runs smoothly. So make up your mind to it that what you say here and now is not a matter of sneaking on your superior. You are compelled by your position to put this situation plainly before me.'

'Yes, Matron!' Andrea nodded slowly. She could see where her duty lay, but she was aware that this could be the start of more trouble than she had ever encountered. She felt that she was out of her depth in this, but Sister Cole had really forced the issues by making a report of the incident which had taken place in the office. Andrea had the strange feeling that events were moving of their own volition, and she was caught up in this involuntarily. It made her aware that she was just another cog in the big machine!

CHAPTER NINE

It was difficult for Andrea to state her case unemotionally. She was under pressure subconsciously because she was not the type to complain or talk about another not in her presence. But she realized that the situation in her department was beginning to get out of hand, and if something were done immediately then a great deal more trouble might be prevented later.

She told Matron of the incidents that had occurred, and even as she narrated them she could tell by her own words that Sister Cole had been unreasonable to an extreme. When she finally lapsed into silence, Matron nodded.

'This is just as I suspected,' she said quietly. 'I had the opportunity to observe Sister Cole when she came here yesterday to make that report about you, and I believe I'm going to have to take some action in this matter. But it must be arranged so that no suspicion of complicity falls upon you, Sister.'

'I certainly don't want Sister Cole to think that I came here to talk about her,' Andrea said. 'It may sound like a good excuse to say it is for the good of the department! But I'm unhappy about this, Matron.'

'I understand, but you can leave it with me. I shall do nothing yet, but you can be sure that I shall learn of everything that takes place in future. Continue in your present attitude. Don't give Sister Cole any cause for complaint, and we'll see what transpires.'

Andrea sighed heavily as she got to her feet. She looked down at her superior, and saw that Matron was nodding slowly.

'I'm glad we had the opportunity for this chat, Sister. It had become obvious to me that it was necessary. I assure you that you've done the right thing. As to the future, we have a new Sister coming into your department on Monday. When the new theatre is ready for use she will head the nurses who will work with Mr Stevens. I understand from Mr Morrell

142

that he will work with no one but you. That's quite a feather in your cap, Sister. Mr Morrell is something of a perfectionist himself, and he praises you highly. Keep up the good work. In view of the atmosphere in your department at the moment I think you are doing very well, and it was most unfortunate that this incident with Mr Stevens took place. But you can be assured that he won't bother you again.'

'Thank you, Matron!' Andrea nodded and departed, and she heaved a long sigh of relief as she walked out of the hospital. Her mind was busy as she entered the car park, and a smile touched her face when she saw Simon's car there.

He got out of the car and opened the passenger door for her, his eyes showing his regard for her, his face wearing an expression of curiosity.

'Well?' he demanded as she slipped into the seat. 'How did it go? Have you been suspended or dismissed for this unknown heinous crime you've committed?'

'No. It wasn't really to do with that, as a matter of fact.' Andrea shook her head slowly. 'I just don't know what to think. Matron has been busy making some enquiries. She mentioned that she has talked to you, and I have the feeling there are a lot of things happening behind the scenes. But she was most concerned about Sister Cole.'

'We're all concerned about Sister Cole,'

143

Simon said thoughtfully. 'I'm beginning to believe that she's becoming mentally deranged.' He went around the car to the driving seat, and Andrea watched his face. When he was seated at her side he looked into her face. 'What shall we do today? I think we're going to find it rare indeed when we'll both be off duty together in future, so let us make the most of this!'

'I'm quite agreeable.' She nodded as she held his gaze. 'But there is one item of news which I learned that you ought to know about. A new Theatre Sister is starting with us on Monday.'

'Cora!' His face became harsh, and his dark eyes narrowed. A sigh escaped him. 'Well she'll have no power at this hospital. Her father doesn't work here. She'll find the difference if she tries to take up here where she left off at the other place.'

His voice was filled with bitterness, his tones thick and almost unrecognizable. Andrea watched him closely, and saw him shake his head.

'She's going to work in the new Theatre when it's opened, and Clifford will be the surgeon.'

'So long as she doesn't work with me,' he said. He sighed again, heavily, and then smiled, as if he had got rid of all the tension that had accumulated inside him at the mention of Cora Bayliss. 'I am ready to leave here. What suggestions have you for spending the day?'

'You're the driver,' she advised. 'I don't know what you like. I'd hate to suggest something which would spoil your day.'

'I like you, and whatever you like is all right by me!' He took hold of her hand and squeezed it gently. 'Let's make it a day to remember, Andrea.'

'It will certainly be that,' she said, smiling. 'I've waited a long time and hoped quite a lot to spend some time in your company.'

'I lay awake last night thinking about last evening,' he said. 'I could hardly believe what you said. It seemed such a miracle. I woke up this morning thinking it had all been a dream, but here we are together, and the sun is shining and everything in the garden is lovely. Isn't it strange how we humans must have relationships? Getting to know you is like having an unexpected treat. When I look at you I can understand the meaning behind our living.'

She saw that he was really serious, and she agreed with his words. Her hopes had been high regarding him, and before yesterday she had felt that something was missing from her life. But now she was complete, and for the first time in her life.

'We're getting really serious!' A smile touched his lips. 'I suggest we take a deep breath, hold it for a moment, and then go on

145

from there!'

'Trying to decide on where to go today,' she retorted.

He chuckled, and she had never seen his face looking younger. He started the car and drove out of the park, and when they were in the stream of traffic he glanced at her.

'Do you have to go home?' he demanded.

'Well it rather depends on what we plan to do!'

'What about a trip to the coast? Would you like a day at the seaside?'

'Swimming?' Her pale green eyes seemed to glow with an inner light. 'That sounds just what the doctor ordered.'

'I know a bit about medicine,' he retorted with a ghost of a smile, 'and I do think you would benefit from just such an excursion.'

'Then I'll have to go home for a towel and my swim suit.'

'Can you swim?'

'Of course! I was almost a schoolgirl champion!' Andrea chuckled light-heartedly.

'Then you can teach me to swim!'

'Can't you?' She showed surprise. 'I rather imagine you can do anything and everything that requires skill.'

'Thank you! But how on earth do I live up to your opinion?' He reached out and took hold of her hand, holding it gently for a moment. 'Oh, the days off duty that I've spent alone, wishing that I could have been with you!

146

You'll never know how much I've wanted to get to know you, Andrea.'

She thought of her own longings of the past, and nodded. She knew exactly what he meant, and she could still hardly believe that the miracle had really occurred.

'I'll drop you off at your home and go on to my flat,' he said suddenly. 'You should be ready to leave by the time I get back to you. I've got some swimming trunks somewhere, and it won't take me long to hunt them up.'

Andrea agreed with his plan, and when she reached home she hurried in to acquaint her mother with it while Simon went off to his flat. Mrs Chaston was surprised by the news, but Andrea could see that her mother was pleased.

'It's about time you found someone, you know,' she said. 'I have been worried about you for a long time.'

'So Father said!' Andrea smiled. 'But I'm normal, Mother! It was just that I never met the right man.'

'And you think Simon is?'

'Oh I don't know about that! It's too early to say.' Andrea was not going to commit herself yet. It was early days, and she knew that the future contained some tense moments for the both of them. Monday would see the arrival of Cora Bayliss, and they would have to wait to see how the woman acted towards Simon.

'You must get Simon to call here often,' Mrs Chaston said. 'I think we'd better try to make him one of the family as quickly as possible.'

'Why do you say that?' Andrea frowned. 'Don't try your hand at match-making, Mother. You might scare him off.'

'You should know me better than that!' Mrs Chaston shook her head. 'I wouldn't interfere in your life, Andrea. You're a very responsible person, and I should give you credit for being able to manage your own life.'

'Thanks.' Andrea nodded slowly. 'I think we're facing a difficult future, Mother, although I'll give you no details. But there are indications that we can expect some rough weather for a time.'

'I'm sorry to hear that. I hope it's not connected with your work.'

'It isn't that, although I am having a tough time of it with Sister Cole at the moment. But from what I learned in Matron's office this morning that may all be ironed out before long.'

'Simon isn't married, is he?' Mrs Chaston held Andrea's eyes for a moment.

'No! It isn't that particular complication, thank Heaven!' Andrea's relief was genuine. 'Perhaps I'm just looking for likely trouble spots and there really isn't anything to worry about. I suppose it's because I feel so elated that I'm instinctively afraid that something will come along and spoil it all.'

'You deserve any happiness that may come your way, my dear!' Mrs Chaston reached out and placed a hand upon Andrea's shoulder. 'I'm sure it will come right for you. Don't cross any bridges until you come to them.'

'I shan't, and I won't count my chickens before they're hatched either,' Andrea said firmly.

She was ready to leave by the time Simon returned, and Mrs Chaston came to the door to see them off. She waved in friendly fashion to Simon, and he replied eagerly. Andrea thought that he was beginning to slip into her family without difficulty, and her lovely face showed her joy as she waved to her mother while Simon turned the car around.

But when they were on the open road and making for the coast Simon looked grave, and Andrea felt her heart seem to skip a beat as she looked at him.

'Is something wrong?' she demanded.

'There was a message waiting for me when I reached the flat. Cora has arrived already. She wants to settle in during the week-end. She pushed a note through my letter box saying that she'd been waiting around for me, having learned at the hospital that I was off duty today, and that she would be calling this afternoon.'

'Well that's nothing to worry about, is it? You'll have to see her and talk to her, Simon. But as soon as you inform her of the situation that exists between us it should put her off.'

'You don't know Cora,' he replied.

Andrea settled back in her seat, determined that nothing should spoil this day, and she dismissed all thoughts of the hospital, Sister Cole and Cora Bayliss from her mind. They were silent on the drive to the coast, speaking occasionally about things in general, but where Andrea's mind was rather clear, Simon seemed to be inwardly worrying about the situation.

They reached the coast just before lunch, and went into a restaurant for a meal. They ate lightly, both wanting to swim as soon as possible, and they went to the crowded beach and settled down amidst the teeming holidaymakers. They spread their towels together, stripped down to their swim suits, and lay on the hot sands for a time.

'This isn't really my idea of taking a quiet trip to the coast,' Simon said. 'Now in Cornwall you can actually find some deserted beaches if you know where to look.'

'That would be a blessing.' Andrea turned on her back and looked around at the holiday crowds. Someone had a transistor radio blaring out, and children were scampering around, kicking sand over people, but everyone was getting full enjoyment.

'Have you made any plans for your holiday this year?' Simon demanded.

'Not yet! Sister Cole never goes away on holiday, and I've not bothered before about when I take my entitlement. How about you?'

'I'm going home to Cornwall in late August!' He propped himself on one elbow and studied her lovely face. Andrea was wearing a red bikini, and she had spent some of her free time sunbathing in the garden at home so she had the makings of a tan. But Simon was pale by contrast, and she realized that he didn't relax very often. 'I know it's a bit early to start making plans, but by the time August gets here we should know each other pretty well. Would you consider taking a week's holiday when I do and coming home with me?'

'I think I'd like that, Simon,' she replied instantly. 'But I don't think it would be wise to start making long term plans.'

'But August is only a couple of months away,' he protested.

'I know, and we have some tricky moments coming up long before August shows on the calendar,' she retorted.

He nodded slowly, holding her gaze, and Andrea got slowly to her feet. She looked down at him. He was tall and slim, with quite an athletic figure. His brown eyes gleamed as they studied her.

'Come along,' she prompted. 'Let's get into the water.'

He leaped to his feet at her words and they raced through the people on the beach to the water's edge. Simon reached the water first, and paused to test it with a cautious toe, but

Andrea bustled straight by him and waded in, wincing involuntarily at her contact with the water, which was cold despite the heat of the day, and then she plunged forward in a shallow dive and came up striking out powerfully. When she turned her head to look for Simon she found him swimming strongly to come up with her.

'This is better,' he flung at her as she trod water some fifty yards out from the shore. 'You can swim extremely well.'

'You're not doing so badly yourself, are you?' she retorted.

'Not for a beginner.' He came close, his teeth glinting as he looked at her with a smile on his face. 'Do you mind if I look at you at length today? I really can't control my impulses. If you gave me the opportunity I would watch you until the sun went down.'

'What's so attractive about me?' she demanded, dashing water out of her eyes and almost going beneath the surface as she did so.

'Take a closer look at yourself in the mirror next time,' he retorted.

'Beauty is only skin deep.' Her pale green eyes seemed to burn with a strange fire as the sunlight caught them in reflection from the calm surface of the sea. One of her arms touched him as she kept herself afloat, and he came even closer, until their faces were almost touching.

'I wish today would never end!' His voice

was husky. Water glistened in his dark, curly hair. He seemed almost a stranger, accustomed as she was to seeing him around the hospital, and she was seeing a side to him that she hadn't dreamed existed.

'I've had that feeling ever since we left the hospital,' she admitted. 'But all good things must come to an end.'

'There will be other times.' He spoke hopefully, and smiled when she nodded.

'I shall be looking forward to them. I think we can decide here and now that I will accompany you to Cornwall when you take your holiday.'

'No matter what happens in the meantime?'

She nodded slowly. 'We must make up our minds at the outset that nothing will be permitted to come between us,' she said thoughtfully. 'If your ex-fiancée is as bad as you say then she's surely going to make some effort to get you veering back to her.'

He smiled tightly, but his eyes were hard with determination. 'That's nothing as far as I'm concerned. She could never succeed in getting me to even look at her twice again. She's as hard as flint inside, Andrea, and you'd better bear that in mind all the time. I think you're the one she will attack when she finds out about us. Have I given you the impression that I'm worried for myself?'

'I didn't know what to think, but what could she do to me? Andrea chuckled at the thought.

'I shall be her superior in the department. We shan't see much of each other, in any case. But she can do me no harm.'

'Knowing her, I hesitate to agree with you. But I shall be watching her very closely, and you'd be well advised to do the same.' He was so very serious, and Andrea frowned as she turned under the water and came up to float upon her back. He came close to her once more, his eyes showing his concern. 'If anything happened to your career because of her I'd never forgive myself.'

'I've got an idea.' Andrea held his gaze. 'Let's forget about Surlington and everything that goes with it until we have to return later, shall we?'

'That sounds like a splendid suggestion.' He smiled, and pulled her over so that they both shot beneath the surface. Andrea managed to fill her lungs with air, and they went down into the greenish depths together. When they came up and broke surface, he kissed her quickly. 'Race you back to the shore,' he said, and started out quickly.

Andrea struck out behind him, and for a time she managed to keep at his side, but he was a powerful swimmer and beat her to the shore. He was standing knee deep in the water when she arose and waded to his side. Putting an arm around her shoulders, Simon led her up the beach to where their clothes lay, and they seemed to be alone amidst the vast crowd that packed the sands. They lay down on their towels, and Simon's right hand touched the back of her neck. She turned her head to look at him, lifting one hand to shield her eyes from the strong sunlight, and he watched her intently.

'I'm certain that I love you, Andrea,' he said softly. 'The past weeks have dragged by and I've been in a fever over you. But since yesterday I've relaxed, knowing that you have some feelings for me.'

'It's strange that we were attracted to one another, and yet knew nothing about it!' She was serious as she held his gaze. 'I always thought you were too serious-minded to have time for such a luxury as romance.'

'Do you think romance is a luxury?' he asked instantly.

'Well we can live without it. Life is rather grey and dull when romance is excluded, and sometimes it doesn't seem to be worth living, but we don't die for the lack of romance.'

'I just didn't want to start anything that might complicate my life or yours,' he retorted. 'After what happened the last time!' He firmed his lips and shook his head. 'Here I go again.'

She smiled. 'I don't mind you talking about it. Perhaps it's what you should have done long ago. If you'd talked about it more it wouldn't have any significance now.'

'You're quite the psychologist! But you're right, of course! But there's nothing to talk about now. It will just die a natural death.'

He put his head close to Andrea's, then kissed her, and she closed her eyes and relaxed, letting her emotions take control and roam at will through her. She found her mind completely easy now, and that seemed miraculous when she thought of the past few days. Sister Cole had been wearing her down, making her nervy and irritable, but it was all gone now, and she didn't think her superior would ever be able to work her up into such a state again.

Thinking of Sister Cole made the interview with Matron return to her thoughts, and she considered everything that had been said, until Simon spoke quietly in her ear.

'Are you asleep?' he asked.

'No!' She opened her eyes and looked at him.

'Then you were thinking about the hospital,' he accused, and she laughed.

The afternoon passed all too quickly, and they bathed several times before they decided they'd had enough. After dressing they went back to the restaurant for tea, and the impressions Andrea picked up would remain vivid in her mind for the rest of her life. However she began to think of returning to Surlington, and she was saddened by the knowledge that reality was ever at their shoulders. When they walked to the car she felt herself tightening up inside, and she could tell by Simon's expression that he was thinking in the same vein.

They drove homewards, and it was still very early evening by the time they sighted the town. Their conversation had dwindled as they continued, until Simon glanced at her.

'I don't want to take you home yet, Andrea,' he said. 'I have a rather nasty feeling that Cora will be around somewhere, like a bad fairy, waiting for me to return home. I rather fancy I'd like to have you along when I do see her.'

'For moral support?' She raised an eyebrow. 'Of course I'll be with you if you wish.'

'If she sees us together she'll get the message a lot quicker than if I just told her about you,' he said.

That sounded like commonsense to Andrea, and she took a deep breath as she settled herself back in her seat. Simon drove towards his flat, and when he reached the tall block which housed a great number of the hospital staff, he pulled into the kerb behind a white Triumph Herald. As he switched off the ignition he caught Andrea's gaze, and his face was taut and bitter as he pointed through the windscreen.

'That's Cora's car now,' he said sharply, 'and she's in it. What did I tell you?'

Andrea sighed sharply, and forced herself to remain outwardly calm. She could see a woman's head and shoulders in the car in front, and she was suddenly trembling as they alighted. Now she would get a measure of this woman who had caused so much trouble for Simon!

CHAPTER TEN

Simon waited for Andrea to join him on the pavement, and his face was expressionless once again. He took her arm, and Andrea felt stronger as she leaned upon his hand, feeling his strength and knowing that he cared about her. The door of the white car was opened and a tall, slim, cool looking blonde alighted, subjecting them to a steady gaze before slamming the door of her vehicle.

'Hello, Simon! I've been waiting around here most of the day to see you. Didn't you get my note?'

Blue eyes regarded Andrea while the words were directed at Simon in level tones.

'I saw your note, but I'm sorry I had made other plans.' Simon's voice gave no indication of his feelings now. 'Before you go any further, Cora, you'd better meet Andrea Chaston. Sister Chaston, Assistant Theatre Superintendent at St. Catherine's, to give her a correct title. Andrea, this is Cora Bayliss! She's coming into your department as a Sister on Monday.'

'How do you do?' Andrea had to make an

effort to make her voice sound natural.

'Hello!' There was no warmth in Cora's voice. Her blue eyes were glittering like ice under lamplight. She was as tall as Andrea, but there was a swing to her slim shoulders, an air of haughtiness about her that warned Andrea for the future. 'I've heard all about you. I spent some time at the hospital this afternoon.'

'You'll hear nothing but praise about Andrea,' Simon said in warning tones.

'I must have been talking to the wrong people today then,' came the swift reply.

'Well what is it you want to see me about?' Simon cut in.

'Do I have to have a special reason for wanting to see you? We're old friends, and we were very special friends not so long ago!' Cora's blue eyes narrowed as she smiled thinly. 'Have you told Andrea all about me?'

'Just about everything there is to know,' Simon said.

The girl's expression hardened, and she met Andrea's gaze boldly, almost insolently. 'I must get together with her and tell her all about you,' she retorted.

'Let's not beat about the bush, or are you getting catty,' Simon went on in smooth tones. He was still holding Andrea's arm, and she was thankful for the support. 'I've been here three months, Cora, and they've been the happiest three months of my life. I don't know why you've suddenly turned up. It can only be

159

because you think you can still twist me around your little finger. But I'm going to tell you at the outset, and only once, that there's no future for us together. You've wasted your time coming here, and you'll only make yourself unhappy if you start your usual tricks around the hospital.'

'You're giving Sister Chaston an unfavourable opinion of me,' Cora said softly.

'She doesn't know you, but I do—only too well.' A hard edge sounded in Simon's voice. 'It's going to be difficult for me working in the same hospital with you, Cora. If you understand here and now that it will be better if we keep as far apart as possible then we should be able to get by. But I know why you've come here, and you are not going to succeed.'

'I expected this attitude at first,' the girl said, unperturbed by his words. 'But give me time to settle in and you'll see the difference.' She met Andrea's eyes, and a thin smile touched her lips, a smile that had nothing to do with friendliness in its taut movement. 'I spoke with Sister Cole this afternoon. She's a very able Sister, I judged.'

'She's the type you'd get on well with,' Simon said. He looked at Andrea. 'If I sound a bit harsh and boorish in my manner then I ask you to forgive me. I can't bring myself to forget what happened, and Cora knows that.'

Andrea said nothing, but Cora laughed

lightly.

'I'll be seeing you on Monday, Sister Chaston,' she said. 'I hope to see you sooner than that, Simon.' She turned then and got back into her car, and Simon and Andrea stood silently until she drove away. Then Simon heaved a long sigh.

'What do you think to her?' he demanded, turning Andrea, still holding her arm, and starting towards the block of flats.

'I don't think she's going to be any great help to the atmosphere that we've got in the department at the moment,' Andrea said cautiously. 'She has quite an attitude, as you told me, and it shows. I can only shudder when I think of her clashing with Sister Cole!'

'I don't like the way she said that she'd talked to Sister Cole this afternoon,' he said slowly. 'If those two gang up on you, Andrea, your life won't be worth living.'

'I'm not worried about that.' Andrea paused as they entered the flats, and Simon pressed a button for a lift.

They entered and ascended several floors, then left the lift and walked along a tiled corridor to one of the flats.

'Well she's here now!' A sigh escaped Simon. 'We could have done without her, certainly, but she is here and she's going to stay. If we're both on our guard all the time then there's nothing much she can do. But promise me you'll be very careful, won't you,

Andrea?'

'I promise!' She smiled confidently, but she was feeling uncertain as she looked into his eyes. He unlocked the door of the flat and they entered, and Simon sighed heavily and opened his arms to her. Andrea uttered a little gasp and hurried into his embrace, and the cold fear that had struck her at sight of Cora Bayliss began imperceptibly to fade as he held her close.

Their remaining hours together during the evening fled all too swiftly. Simon made some coffee, and then they sat together in the small lounge, enjoying their company and trying to push the intruding thoughts of Cora out of their minds. Andrea thrilled at Simon's touch, but something was gone from their surrounding atmosphere, and Andrea knew that the abrasive quality of Cora's manner was to blame. She began to dread Monday's arrival, when the girl would arrive on duty. She had the uncanny feeling that what she had thought in the past to be trouble would subsequently be proved as the calm before the real storm, but she took care not to let Simon see her trepidation. This was something else that she would have to fight alone.

When it was time for Simon to take her home, Andrea felt a pang of regret that their time together had come to an end. She was silent on the drive to her home, and when Simon brought the car to a halt in the drive before the house, she turned to him and reached out, searching for his hand.

'Thank you for such a wonderful time,' she said softly. 'I can't remember a day I've enjoyed more. It's been so wonderful with you, just like a dream that's come true.'

'Then there's some hope that we'll be able to repeat the medicine?' His face was just a shapeless blur in the darkness. His teeth glinted as he smiled, and Andrea gripped his hand tightly.

'Whenever we can,' she responded.

'That's all I need to know to keep me going strongly now,' he said.

'You're really worried about Cora's arrival, aren't you?' For a moment she was aware of his deep concern, and it made her think about the girl. Ought she to take Cora seriously? She felt that the strength of her own feelings for Simon, and his for her, would see them through anything the girl might try. But she could not overlook the fact that Cora's presence here in Surlington proved just how determined the girl was.

'I am worried,' he admitted. 'She's already made a great impact on my life. Most people have limits on their patterns of behaviour, but not Cora! The fact that she let a patient die because my absence would spoil her engagement party shows you the kind of thing I mean. So watch out for tricks, Andrea! I really mean that.'

'I'll be careful,' she promised, and sighed heavily. 'Now I suppose I've got to go in. We're both on duty tomorrow.'

'There's nothing scheduled. It's a case of being on hand for emergencies,' he said, and leaned towards her and kissed her lightly.

Andrea put her arms around his neck and clung to him, closing her eyes and letting her mind go blank as her feelings rioted. When they parted she was breathless, thrilled to the very core, and she got unsteadily from the car and stepped back, watching until he had departed. When she was alone she stood in the silence of the night, her mind struggling to settle, her hands trembling as she considered the changes that had been thrust upon her. But she was certain of one thing as she turned slowly to go into the darkened house. If Cora Bayliss was going to make a try to regain Simon's love, then the girl would find she had a tough fight upon her hands . . .

That week-end proved to be long and filled with suspense for Andrea. She went into the hospital on duty on Saturday, and found enough to do to keep herself and the duty nurse busy until lunch time. Simon came into the department, and warned her, just before lunch, that they would have an appendectomy to perform during the afternoon. He remained watching her after giving her the message, and Andrea looked into his dark eyes and let her mind relax into the precious memories of the day before.

'What a really beautiful girl you are!' He narrowed his eyes as he stared at her.

'I'm glad you think so, but beauty is in the eye of the beholder. Perhaps I'm not really beautiful at all. It's just you who thinks so.'

'Well that may be, but it's good enough for me. Can I take you out this evening?'

'I'm on stand-by—first call. Sister Cole is off duty all week-end. I'll be around all the time.'

'I see. Then I'll spend as much time as I can around here. You won't mind me talking to you, will you?'

'I'll be happy to have you around!'

He nodded, and took her arm as they left the office to go to lunch. He drove her home, and then set off for his flat, and Andrea knew she was deeply in love with him. Now the excitement of finally getting together with him was settling inside her, she could view the situation with equanimity, and she liked what she discovered in her mind.

But Saturday passed, and Sunday came. She did not go into the hospital during the morning, but was called just after lunch with news of an emergency. By the time she got to the hospital the standby team was ready, and Simon, working with Clifford Stevens, performed the operation. Afterwards, when the patient had been returned to the ward and the nurses were busy cleaning the theatre, Andrea went to Simon's side. He was talking to Stevens, and she waited nearby until their conversation came to an end. She had no intention of overhearing their conversation, but she heard Stevens talking animatedly.

'I've met the new Sister we've got joining us tomorrow, Simon. She's a real smasher, isn't she? I understand that you and she knew each other before!'

'I know her!' Simon turned and looked at Andrea. 'When you're through here, Andrea, I'll drive you home,' he said.

She nodded, and saw Stevens frown as he glanced at her. Surprise showed in Stevens' eyes, and for a moment he forgot to be sheepish in front of her. She met his gaze, a smile on her lips.

'I shan't be long, Simon,' she replied.

'I'd better get the operation report written up or I won't be ready for you,' Simon said, and he departed quickly, leaving Andrea facing Stevens.

'How long has this been going on?' Clifford demanded his face heavy now, his dark eyes filled with an unfathomable expression.

'What's that?' she demanded innocently.

'You're going around with Simon!'

'Why not? He's free and so am I!'

'But I've been asking you to go out with me for weeks!'

'That's got nothing to do with it. A girl can choose her own company, surely!'

His face changed expression, and for a

166

moment Andrea was certain that he positively hated her. Then he composed himself, frowning, shaking his head.

'I get it,' he said. 'You've been carrying a torch for the big man ever since he came here! I was a fool not to have noticed.'

'It would have saved the both of us a lot of trouble if you had been more observant,' she agreed.

'Do you know about him and Sister Bayliss?'

'I do! I've already met her.'

'Well I haven't had much time to talk to her, but from what I gather, she doesn't intend to let Simon slip through her fingers. That's why she's here.'

'I'm afraid she lost him before he came here. Nothing she can do will make him change his mind about her.' Andrea smiled slowly. 'I don't expect she told you the reason why they split up.'

'What was the reason?' He stared boldly into her face.

Andrea shook her head. 'It's none of my business, and I'm sure it's none of yours, Clifford.'

He was silent for a moment, humour obviously gone, but he made an effort to appear unconcerned.

'I haven't had the chance to ask you how you got on with Matron on Friday!'

'It passed over, as it deserved to. I

understand Sir Humphrey spoke to you! I'm sure you won't do anything so stupid again!'

His face hardened, and she saw a tense light shine in his dark eyes. 'I'm still in love with you,' he said softly, glancing around to ensure that they were not being overheard. 'The fact that you may be getting ideas about Simon doesn't make my situation any different. I can't turn off my emotions like a tap. I'd do anything to make you love me, Andrea.'

'It's impossible to make someone love you,' she pointed out. 'I am sorry about this situation, I really am, but it's out of my control. What can I do about it?'

'You could give me a chance! Let me prove to you how much I love you!'

'It wouldn't help at all, and might make you feel even worse. The only thing you can do is forget about me.'

'Better to tell me to forget how to breathe,' he retorted, and turned on his heel and strode quickly away.

Andrea let her breath exhale in a long sigh, and she shook her head as the swing doors closed behind his departing figure. She felt sorry for him! If he had fallen in love with her then he needed sympathy, because she knew she could never feel anything for him. If Simon hadn't come along she wouldn't have turned to Clifford Stevens.

She was thoughtful as she returned to her work, and when the theatre had been restored to its customary standard of cleanliness and readiness she walked along to the locker room and changed back into her uniform. As she reached the office, Simon appeared from the surgeon's room and came towards her.

Andrea studied his face as he came up, and she could feel a shaft of delight in her mind. The knowledge that he cared for her seemed to fill her with a strange elation. She felt uplifted, borne higher than she had ever imagined it possible for feelings to rise. This was love! The thought touched her awareness. This was what living was all about.

'Ready?' he demanded softly, and the very tones of his voice seemed to caress her.

'Give me a few moments,' she said, holding his gaze. They were standing very close, and she could feel a tingling inside, as if she were metal and he had some kind of magnetism that attracted her physically.

'I do believe you're getting more beautiful each time I see you!' There was a soft smile on his lips, and his expression was gentle. She needed no more proof that he loved her. He sighed heavily then, and she quickly felt alarm.

'Is anything wrong?' she demanded.

'Wrong?' He nodded slowly as he looked intently into her pale eyes. 'There's quite a lot wrong, but I can't do anything about it. However we're on our guard and so we might scrape through without trouble.'

'You're talking about Cora again,' she said,

169

and felt strangely deflated as she mentioned the girl's name.

'I'm sorry if I seem to have a one-track mind where she is concerned, but I know her only too well. The only regret in my mind at this moment is that tomorrow will surely come.'

'I'm looking forward to all our tomorrows,' she countered.

'It's a good thing one of us is an optimist,' he retorted.

Simon took Andrea home, and stayed with her for a time. But they parted later and she went back to the hospital for a couple of hours in the evening. She brought her paperwork up to date, knowing that Sister Cole would be at her if anything had been left undone, and then she went on a tour of the silent theatres, her mind calm, her nerves steady. She found nothing out of place, and went along the new corridor to the new theatre. The builders had finished and some of the equipment had been installed. It would be a week or so before the theatre was commissioned, but when it came into operation the flow of patients would be increased. The staff in the department would be a third as large again, and Andrea wondered how Sister Cole would react to the changes. She hoped that with so much more to do, her superior wouldn't find the time to pursue her policy of hatred.

Retracing her steps, Andrea returned to the office, and she stiffened as she entered, for there was someone seated by the desk. It was Cora Bayliss, and the girl turned to face her as Andrea paused on the threshold.

'I learned that you were here,' the girl said. 'I want to have a talk with you, Sister!'

'Certainly!' Andrea stifled her first reactions and moved to the desk and sat down. 'What's on your mind?'

'You're not busy, are you? Cora was smiling easily, her face composed and showing nothing more than interest.

'Not right now. I'm on duty, and rather than sit at home I thought I'd bring everything up to date. There's nothing like starting a new week with nothing left over from the past.'

'I'm not one to beat around the bush.' The smile faded from Cora's lips, and her blue eyes turned icy for a moment as she fixed Andrea with a stare. 'I don't know how much Simon told you about me, and I don't care what situation exists between the two of you. But I do want you to know that he belongs to me, and I don't intend to let him go. I've been asking questions around the hospital today, and I've learned a lot about you. It's only this week-end that you started going out with Simon. I don't think you two are in love at all. I believe you're just someone Simon has got to stand in with him to help put me off.'

'How wrong can you get?' Andrea countered, smiling. 'I'm afraid you're in for a disappointment if you think you can win

171

Simon again, and I don't consider myself in that statement at all. From what I've heard him say about you I'd say he despises you. How can you beat that?'

'I can find a way around him,' came the sharp reply. 'But I don't want you getting in the way. If you stopped seeing him then he'd turn to me.'

'I'm sorry again, but I have no intention of staying away from him. I happen to be in love with him, and I'm not ashamed to admit it. I would do anything for Simon, and his happiness comes before mine. If I thought you could make him happy then I'd gladly get out of his life. But you've already proved to be a disaster to him, and I feel sure you'll do the same thing again. If you had any feelings at all for him you wouldn't have come here.'

'Is that so?' Cora was smiling again. 'There are different kinds of love, you know. I can see that yours is the selfless kind! Well I don't go in for that sort of thing. I demand! I need more out of love than I put into it, and I think a man likes it that way too! Men are made to provide.'

'You asked too much of Simon,' Andrea retorted, shaking her head. 'You weren't satisfied with his love. You wanted his pride and his skill subjected to your love. That would never work out. Why don't you leave him alone?'

'I told you he's mine, and I'm going to have

him, come what may. You've got a fight on your hands, Sister, and I can't see you winning. I know Simon better than you, and if you'll take my advice you won't make this too difficult for him by trying to hang on to him.'

'I admire your nerve!' Andrea permitted a smile to touch her lips. 'But that's all you've got, Sister! It isn't enough, you know.'

'Well we'll see!' Cora got to her feet, and there was a strange smile on her face. 'I thought it better that we should clear the air about us. We both know where we stand. You think you're right and I know I am. But there's no need for us to be enemies! I'm coming here to do a job, and what happens in our personal lives has nothing to do with the hospital.'

'I agree with that wholeheartedly,' Andrea responded. She was finding some facets of this girl's character very engaging. It was difficult to tie up her instinctive judgement and Simon's opinion. But she realized that Cora Bayliss was deep mentally, and there was a sharpness in her pale blue eyes that belied the manner she was projecting. There lay the seat of her power, Andrea decided. Cora had the ability to conceal her real character. In that way she made rivals underestimate her, and that was a warning Simon had made most plain.

'Then we understand each other!' Cora turned to the door. 'See you tomorrow morning, Sister! I understand the new theatre

173

won't be ready for a week or so. No doubt I shall stand in for you and Sister Cole until my own place is ready.'

'That's up to Sister Cole. No doubt she'll want to find out for herself just what you know.'

'Hasn't Simon told you that I'm the best there is?' A quick smile touched the girl's lips, and before Andrea could reply, Cora departed.

Andrea sat stiffly, listening to the girl's receding footsteps. Full silence returned and she straightened, heaving a long sigh as she did so. Now she had a better idea of what she was up against. Cora Bayliss was filled with feline cunning. She had sharp claws which she kept sheathed against the right moment to use them. There was another side to her which didn't show, and Andrea could sense it. The knowledge was disturbing. It lay in Andrea's mind like a dark shadow, intangible, ominous and very real.

But Andrea had no illusions now. Until this meeting with Cora she had been deluding herself, believing that Simon's experiences with the girl had made him exaggerate a little, but now she knew differently, and she vowed then and there that she would not relax her guard for a moment. She had the uncanny feeling that the first opportunity she offered Cora to score over her would be snatched without compunction, and the girl knew only one way to play the game of living. There were no rules but those which she made for her own advantage. All was fair, especially in love, and Cora knew it.

Andrea mentally girded herself for trouble, and as she departed for home on that peaceful Sunday evening she felt that she was indeed standing upon the threshold of a new phase of her life, a phase that would know more love than she had ever expected, and more experience than she ever believed would be possible.

CHAPTER ELEVEN

Monday morning found Andrea dreading the thought of going on duty, although she dressed and breakfasted as usual and there were no outward signs of difference anywhere in her manner or appearance. She left home and caught her bus, and when she alighted at the hospital gates she found herself breathing heavily, as if she had run all the way from her home. She steeled herself for what she expected to be an ordeal, entered the hospital, and walked to her department.

Her mind was filled with a great many mental notes. She had to follow Matron's orders and continue normally, trying not to give Sister Cole any room for discontent, and she was only too aware that Cora Bayliss was going to make a great impact on the department, no matter what happened.

She neared the office, and paused when she heard the sound of raised voices coming from inside. A cold hand seemed to clutch at her heart as she recognized Simon's voice as one of them, and she was trembling as she pushed open the door and entered.

The first thing she saw was Cora Bayliss seated at her desk, and Andrea firmed her lips. She had instinctively expected the newcomer to try and take over her place. But Simon was standing in front of Sister Cole's desk, and Sister Cole was looking up at him with dogged determination showing in her face and eyes. They both looked round at Andrea, and she saw Simon moisten his lips.

'Good morning,' Andrea said generally.

'Good morning, Andrea,' Simon replied, but neither Sister Cole nor Cora Bayliss replied. Sister Cole glanced at her watch, but Andrea knew she was not late, and she was well accustomed to her superior's manner. She went across to her desk, and Cora Bayliss got to her feet, nodding slightly as they looked into one another's eyes.

'There is no point in continuing this argument,' Simon said brusquely, and his tones were thick with suppressed anger. 'I am not going to work with Sister Bayliss while Sister Chaston is on duty.'

Andrea caught her breath at his words, and she saw a thin smile touch Cora's lips.

'We have to find out just what Sister Bayliss can do,' Sister Cole rapped angrily.

'Then I suggest she works with Sir Humphrey while you watch her,' Simon retorted.

'Sir Humphrey wouldn't agree to that.' It was easy to see that Sister Cole had no intention of letting Cora anywhere near the senior surgeon.

'I'll have a word with Sir Humphrey about it,' Simon said, and he turned on his heel and departed, without so much as a backward glance as he opened the door.

'Well!' Sister Cole drew a shuddering breath. 'I've never come across such behaviour before. I'm sure Sir Humphrey will back me up. But Mr Morrell has overstepped the mark this time. He's been getting worse lately!' She glared at Andrea as if it were her fault.

'We can't really blame him, Sister,' Cora said, moving to the side of Sister Cole's desk. 'I did know Mr Morrell before he came here. We are old friends, in fact. There was some personal trouble between us in the past. It's only natural that he wouldn't want to get to know me too well again.'

'Everyone knows that the moment a nurse comes on duty then all personal matters are forgotten. That applies to surgeons too! I'm not going to have the routine of the whole department upset just because Mr Morrell feels that he doesn't want to work with you, Sister. In fact I think it's a good idea if the teams were changed around every so often. It prevents us from getting too accustomed to certain ways of working.'

Andrea said nothing. She took up the day's operating list and glanced at it, then got to her feet.

'Where are you going?' Sister Cole demanded roughly, and her dark eyes seemed to pierce Andrea.

'Into Theatre. I have to get ready for the first case.' Andrea kept her tones unemotional and impersonal.

'I haven't given instructions yet!' There was an ominous note now in Sister Cole's voice. 'You're not jumping to conclusions, are you, Sister?' She glared at Andrea. 'I want Sister Bayliss to take your place this morning.'

'But Mr Morrell is refusing to work with her!' Andrea suppressed a sigh.

'That matter isn't settled yet! I'm going to have a word with Sir Humphrey myself!'

'But my theatre can't wait until you've sorted this matter out, Sister,' Andrea insisted. 'I suggest that Sister Bayliss goes into the theatre with me and I'll show her the routine, or watch her doing it.'

'Very well.' There was grudging agreement in Sister Cole's harsh voice. 'But don't think that you can start usurping my authority around here, Sister. Just because Mr Morrell acts childish! I won't stand for any nonsense.'

Andrea said nothing, but she looked at the half-smiling Cora. 'If you'd come with me, Sister,' she said curtly.

'Certainly.' Cora accompanied her to the door, and they went out to the corridor. 'You're not on very good terms with Sister Cole, are you?' Cora went on as they walked away from the office. 'She's a bit of a tartar, isn't she?'

'She's strict, but a very good Theatre Sister!' Andrea refused to be drawn.

'But she positively hates you,' Cora insisted.

'I never let personal feelings get the better of me when I'm on duty,' Andrea retorted.

'It's a pity that Sister Cole can't practise what she preaches!' came the quick retort, and Andrea mentally agreed. 'Have you had much trouble with her?'

'I don't class it as trouble! She's just over-zealous, that's all.' Andrea had no intention of revealing the true state of affairs that existed in the department, and there was no further opportunity to talk. They entered the theatre, and Andrea introduced Cora to the nurses. Cora soon showed that she was a very good theatre sister herself, and Andrea supervised her work as she took over the routine of preparing for the first case.

Clifford Stevens came into the theatre. Smiling, he came across to greet Cora, and he hardly took any notice of Andrea at all, which relieved her. Andrea withdrew and quickly continued with the final preparations. She checked everything and was satisfied that everything was ready. Then the swing doors opened and Sister Cole appeared in the doorway. Andrea spotted her superior and walked towards her.

'I don't want you,' Sister Cole retorted rudely. 'Tell Sister Bayliss that she'll be with me in my theatre today.'

Andrea nodded and turned away, realizing that Simon had got his way in the dispute, and she didn't like the expression that showed on Sister Cole's face. The woman was burning inside with anger and frustration. Informing Sister Bayliss, Andrea saw a momentary lapse of expression on the woman's part. But Cora soon recovered her poise and departed with a smile.

A few moments later Simon came into the theatre with the RSO, and his face showed the state of his feelings. He softened a little when he caught Andrea's eye, and a smile flitted across his lips, but he was upset, and Andrea felt a prickling of presentiment as she considered. This was the kind of atmosphere Cora would want to exist in the department, she felt, and knew the woman would soon attempt to make capital from all the stresses and human emotions that were involved. But she thought ruefully that there was little Cora could do to make Sister Cole any worse.

The morning passed without further incident, and Andrea was glad when they stopped for lunch. She supervised the cleaning of the theatre for the afternoon's list, and then went along to the office. She heard voices as she opened the door, and found Sister Cole and Cora chatting comfortably when she entered. Cora smiled at her without friendliness in her expression, and Sister Cole just stared.

'How are you doing with your list?' Sister Cole demanded. 'I suppose you're behind, as usual.'

'Not too far behind,' Andrea countered.

'I've had quite a job to work out the stand-by duties so that Sister Bayliss and Mr Morrell don't get together.' Sister Cole looked at Andrea as if inviting comment. 'I really don't know what all the fuss is about. From what I've seen of Sister Bayliss this morning she's a very efficient and competent nurse. It's too bad that our surgeons have to start getting temperamental.'

Andrea moved to her desk without comment, and Cora Bayliss arose to let her sit down. Andrea made some notes, and Sister Cole spoke again, sharply.

'You could have the decency to look at me and give me the whole of your attention while I'm talking to you, Sister.'

'I'm sorry. I thought you had finished. I

have to make these notes, and we're due back in theatre very shortly. I must hurry to lunch and get back again as soon as possible. The stand-by list isn't so important. I can always see it, and I don't mind what day or evenings you've put me down for.'

There was nothing for Sister Cole to get upset about in Andrea's words, and the woman shook her head slowly as Andrea got to her feet once more.

'I don't know what this department is coming to,' Sister Cole retorted. Her lips were thin and twisted, and her eyes were showing great emotion. Andrea paused to look at her, and she was a little shocked by the amount of emotion that seemed to be running through her superior. But she realized that Sister Cole had come off second best that morning against Simon, and that would have some effect upon her. 'I can remember when Sister's word was law! But times change. Some girls get responsibility and they're not ready for it. Some of the Sisters of today wouldn't get anywhere if they'd had to gain promotion in the conditions that prevailed when I worked my way up.'

'Sisters of today have to learn a great deal more than the Sisters of yesterday,' Andrea countered as she moved to the door.

'Knowledge isn't everything! Perhaps you'll grasp that fact one of these days.'

'I'm sure you're quite right!' Andrea
182

opened the door, and found Simon standing outside. She hurriedly departed and closed the door, looking enquiringly at Simon as she did so.

'I didn't want to come in where Sister Cole is,' he said quietly. 'I could hear her voice inside. Was she getting on to you again?'

'That's nothing new! I'm getting so I hardly notice it now. Is there something you wanted?'

'I've got to make a change in this afternoon's list. I want to bring one case forward. But we can talk about that over lunch. You're not planning on going home, are you?'

'No. I don't usually go home. There is never enough time. I eat at a little restaurant just along the street from here.'

'I know. I've seen you going there. I'll join you if I may. I have the feeling that I may be traced to where I usually go, and I don't want to be unpleasant in any way. I've had enough of that already today.' He smiled thinly. 'If I'm in your company there won't be any chance of a certain person gatecrashing my table and my company.'

'Very well!' Andrea looked at her watch. 'But time is getting away, Simon. We'll have to hurry.'

As they walked along the corridor together the office door was opened and Sister Cole and Cora emerged. Andrea could hear their voices, and her pulses raced as she heard Sister

Cole make some remark. But Simon took no notice and they left the hospital and walked along the street to the restaurant.

After lunch, they walked back to the hospital, and Andrea was glad that she didn't have to see Sister Cole. There was a copy of the duty roster on her desk, and she checked the dates and times of her stand-by duties. Sister Cole had been scrupulously fair in allotting the periods, and Andrea saw no room for complaint. It pleased her that she would be on duty when Simon was on call, and that they would be off duty together. She went into theatre to prepare for the afternoon session, and when she spoke to Simon before they commenced she discovered that they had the same day off duty during the week.

'Let's hope our luck holds like this,' he said, smiling as he pulled up his mask, and Andrea tied it into position for him. 'Now let's get started so we can get done and away. Am I seeing you this evening?'

'Yes please,' she said in a small voice, and he chuckled.

But they found complications in one case, and by the time they finished for the day the evening was nearly past. Andrea was tired as they cleared up, and when she went along to the office she found Cora Bayliss there. The woman was on first call, and she was seated at Sister Cole's desk.

'You've had a long day,' she remarked

pleasantly as Andrea went into the office.

'We would have been finished earlier but we had trouble in one case,' Andrea replied, sitting down rather heavily at her desk. 'How did you get on today?'

'Very well indeed. I had Sister Cole breathing down my neck most of the time, but I think I've satisfied her that I'm quite as capable as she.' There was a sharp tone in the woman's voice that made an impression on Andrea. 'However she's left me alone this evening. I think she'll come around to my way of thinking in a very short time.'

'Your way of thinking?' Andrea queried.

The door opened before Cora could reply, and Simon appeared. He was smiling as he came into the office, but Andrea saw his face change the instant he set eyes on Cora.

'What are you doing here?' he asked her instantly.

'I'm on first call, so I thought I'd stick around to familiarize myself with everything. I am a new girl here, remember.'

He nodded. Andrea was watching him closely, and she saw that he felt uneasy in Cora's presence, but the girl seemed to be enjoying the situation.

'Are you ready to leave, Andrea?' he asked, looking towards her, and she nodded and got to her feet. She saw that Cora's face had hardened at his words, and although the smile was still on the woman's face it was a mere

185

shadow of an expression.

'Yes.' Andrea got to her feet, and she suppressed a sigh. 'Goodnight, Sister,' she said as she walked towards the door.

'Goodnight,' came the even reply, and they departed.

'Well that's the first day over,' Simon said as they left the hospital and walked towards his car. 'What did it seem like to you?'

'It didn't go so badly. In fact it was better than I thought it might be. But if you hadn't stood up to Sister Cole this morning we would have had Cora with us all day and every day until her own theatre is ready.'

'That was something I wasn't going to stand for,' he retorted. 'But she didn't think I would have a word with Sir Humphrey himself. I had to tell him exactly what happened before I came here, and he agreed instantly with me. He thought Cora's presence in theatre while I was operating would prove too much of a distraction. But of course he had to take my side in this.'

Andrea knew it wasn't just the result of a petty thought that had made him refuse to have Cora in his team. After what had happened between them it was obvious to anyone with any knowledge of the tensions of a Theatre that Cora should not be permitted within a mile of Simon unless there was an emergency. But Sister Cole didn't see it that way, and Andrea knew the incident of the

186

morning had only served to worsen the situation that existed, and to sharpen Sister Cole's attitude.

They drove out of the car park, and Andrea settled back in the seat and closed her eyes. She was exhausted. The hours had dragged by and she was both physically and mentally worn out. There was strain inside her. She felt like someone living on the brink of a precipice, someone afraid of heights. Disaster could only be a stone's throw away in her life, she told herself as she began to doze, and she sighed heavily and straightened, opening her eyes again. She glanced at Simon to find a smile on his lips, and when she questioned him he smiled more widely.

'I'd just looked at you,' he said. 'You do work hard, Andrea. The hours are long, aren't they?'

'I've gotten used to that, but it isn't work so much or the hours. Sister Cole makes everything seem so very much harder.'

'You said something about Matron watching Sister Cole!'

'That's what she said, or words to that effect. What will happen I just don't know.' Andrea sighed.

'Well if it doesn't get any worse than it was today we shan't grumble,' Simon said, bringing the car to a halt before her house. 'I can take it if you can.'

She nodded, smiling. 'Are you coming in?'

she demanded.

'You look too tired to entertain,' he countered. 'Why don't you go in and have an early night?'

'Don't you want to spend any time with me?' She suddenly found a picture in her mind of Cora Bayliss sitting alone at the hospital, and she caught her breath and shook her head. 'But you must be tired too, Simon. Don't let me be selfish and keep you if you would rather go home.'

'Not me!' He moved closer. 'We've been pretty close all day, but I haven't been able to say the things I've wanted to say, or relax in your company. We're going to have to snatch what time we can, you know.'

'I'm only too aware of it. I'm on duty all day tomorrow, and I shall be in the office until ten at least tomorrow evening. We shan't see much of one another.'

'I'm standing by tomorrow evening, so I'll come and spend the time with you, if you don't mind,' he said. 'I'm not going to give Cora any chance of getting me into a position which I might find difficult to escape from.'

'Are you afraid of her, Simon? Does she still have any power over you?'

He looked startled for a moment, and the shadows that were creeping into the interior of the car almost hid his expression.

'What I mean is, are you still a little bit in love with her?' Andrea watched his face intently, her hands clenched.

'I was never in love with her,' he replied slowly. 'I thought I was, but after I realized that I wasn't I discovered that I hadn't been even halfway in love with her. I despise her, Andrea! That's saying a lot for me, but it's the truth. I really despise her!'

'I'm sorry I asked, but I have to be sure! You were almost engaged to her, and that dreadful incident which broke it up between you might just have smothered your feelings. It was quite possible that seeing her again after a period of three months might have brought it home to you.'

'Perhaps that is what she's hoping will happen!' He spoke softly, thoughtfully, and his hand crept out and took hold of hers. 'If that is the case then she's doomed to disappointment. You've got me in your hands, Andrea, and I couldn't wish for better.'

She smiled, then stifled a yawn, and he squeezed her hand.

'It's getting late,' he said. 'You'd better go in and get to bed early. We've got two major operations scheduled for tomorrow, and I have to assist Sir Humphrey tomorrow afternoon. He's got a really tricky job on. I wonder if Sister Cole will get you in on it or take Cora? I've got a feeling that Cora will try to use Sister Cole's attitude to you to her own advantage. Be careful there, Andrea. Don't let Cora fool you into a false sense of security.'

'I won't,' she promised, and slipped into his arms. 'If you won't come into the house now then let's spend a little time together out here.'

His arms closed tightly around her and seemed to convey a sense of security with their strength. Andrea gave a little sigh as she relaxed against him, and then he kissed her and filled her veins with fire. Reality seemed to fade, and for the first time that day Andrea felt her tension slipping away. She closed her eyes and lay limply in his embrace, and she fancied she could hear the beating of her heart, although it was the blood pounding in her temples. But her heart was beating for him, and nothing would ever be able to change that, she told herself remotely. They had been destined to meet and to fall in love, and all the Cora Baylisses in the world wouldn't be able to do anything about it.

But time would tell, she realized, and as she left Simon a little later, Andrea found herself wishing that a month could pass quickly, taking with it the uncertainties and fears which lay hidden and dangerous in the long days just ahead. She had the feeling that if she could get through the next month without serious trouble then they would have a very good chance of riding out the gathering storm which seemed to be rising about them . . .

CHAPTER TWELVE

The ensuing days did seem to speed up a little to Andrea's mind. But they were greatly overworked, and most of the time on duty was spent in the operating theatres. Cora Bayliss slipped into the routines at St Catherine's with the ease of a skilled nurse, which she was, and Sister Cole seemed to lean mentally towards the new Sister. It seemed to Andrea that Sister Cole needed support in her strange campaign of hatred against her, and Cora Bayliss was an opportunist who would not miss such a golden chance of gaining allies in whatever it was she intended. But as the days slipped by without major trouble, Andrea began to feel that there was no danger. She wanted peace desperately, and was inclined to close her eyes to the small signs that were ever present whenever she came into contact with Sister Cole.

A week passed, and Andrea was off duty over the week-end. She finished at the hospital on Friday evening at ten and went home with the knowledge that she would not return to duty until Monday morning. Simon was not on duty, and had left the hospital at six. Andrea went home on the bus, and when she arrived she found her mother waiting for her. Mrs Chaston seemed worried, and Andrea had a faint suspicion that something was wrong.

191

'It's Peter Barlow,' her mother told her. 'He hasn't been seen around since his mother's funeral, and the police entered the house a short time ago and found him dead.'

'Dead!' Andrea felt herself turning cold, and she clutched at her mother's arm as she felt her senses whirl. 'What happened to him? Was he ill?'

'He committed suicide!' Mrs Chaston shook her head sadly. 'I can't tell you how I felt when I heard the news. It was the most dreadful thing I ever heard.'

'Poor Peter!' Andrea moved to a chair and sat down rather heavily, her mind spinning. She pictured Peter Barlow's face as she had seen it that early morning before his mother's fatal operation, and again afterwards when he had learned of Mrs Barlow's death. He had seemed so grief stricken and lonely! He had needed help, and she hadn't noticed it because she had been so taken up with Simon! Her conscience troubled her at that moment, but she knew it was too late for remorse. She looked up into her mother's face, and hardly saw the expression there. All she could see was Peter's face as it had looked on the day his mother died.

'I knew it would be a shock to you, Andrea,' Mrs Chaston said.

'How did he die?' Andrea asked.

'He hanged himself!'

Andrea closed her eyes and breathed

deeply, trying to overcome the cold shudders that passed through her. She could almost hear Mrs Barlow's voice in her mind when she had visited the woman just before she had been due to visit the theatre.

'I ought to have found some time to find out how Peter was making out,' Andrea said dully. 'I knew he was taking it badly. That day his mother died! He came to the hospital later to talk to me. Oh, how I wish I could have helped him! But I thought he would get over it.'

'You wouldn't have been able to do anything for him,' Mrs Chaston said softly. 'Don't start blaming yourself for this, Andrea. You do more than your share for humanity. Your work is very demanding. Look at you now! You've been at the hospital all day, and I don't suppose you had five minutes to yourself from the time you entered the place.'

'That's not the point!' Andrea sighed sharply. 'A few words at the right time to Peter might have diverted him. But it's too late now!'

'I feel dreadful about it. I did go to the funeral,' Mrs Chaston said. 'I did remark how ill and strained Peter looked. But I never dreamed he would do such a thing.'

Andrea shook her head slowly. 'It's a bad business! Peter lived for his mother!'

'They were all alone in the world! They lived for each other. She worried herself sick over him and he worried over her. Poor boy!

But he's out of his misery now! That's the only way to look at it, Andrea. He's past his trouble.'

Andrea nodded and got slowly to her feet. She sighed sharply as she went to the door of the room. 'I'm going to bed, Mother,' she said. 'Goodnight.'

'Won't you have some supper before you go? Can I get you something to drink?'

'Nothing thank you. All I want to do is sleep!'

'Perhaps you'd better take a tablet tonight! You look overtired, and this shocking news won't help you find rest.'

'I'd rather not, thank you. See you in the morning, Mother.' Andrea kissed her mother's cheek with stiff lips and then went up to her room. She prepared to go to bed, and fancied that she would be unable to sleep, but as soon as her head touched the pillow her great weariness triumphed over her shocked mind, and she slipped away easily into slumber . . .

It was raining next morning when she awoke, and Andrea slipped out of bed to go to the window. She stared out at a grey day, and sight of the heavily laden clouds scudding across the sky filled her with a great despondency. She found her mind sombre, her attitude taut and serious, and she could not get her thoughts from Peter Barlow.

But she kept her seriousness to herself when she went down to breakfast, although she was aware that her mother studied her very carefully. They ate their meal in near silence, with Mrs Chaston keeping what little conversation there was to general topics.

'What are you going to do without Simon around this week-end, Andrea?' Mrs Chaston asked suddenly.

'I thought of doing some shopping but I'm not going out in that weather,' Andrea replied. 'I think I'll go into the hospital to see Simon. He'll be on duty all day, and he said he had some paperwork to catch up on. I feel the need to talk to him.'

'You'd better borrow my umbrella or you'll be soaked before you get to the bus stop,' her mother retorted.

Andrea felt the need to get out of the house, and she dearly wanted to talk to Simon. She found the weather improving by the time she went up to her room after breakfast, and that finally decided her to make the trip to the hospital. By the time she was ready the rain had stopped completely and the sun was trying to break through the ragged clouds. She felt her spirits lift imperceptibly as she set out for the bus stop.

When she arrived at the hospital she entered cautiously, not wanting to run into either Sister Cole or Cora Bayliss. Sister Cole was on duty all week-end, having had the previous week-end free, and Cora Bayliss would be in the new theatre, preparing for its first operation on the coming Monday. Andrea knew Sister Cole would be in the office, or somewhere around the department. Sister Cole was always on duty!

But she had to pass the Theatre Superintendent's office to get to the surgeons' room, and Andrea was tense as she walked swiftly along the corridor. She heard voices in the office as she went by, and a tight little smile touched her lips as she recognized Sister Cole's harsh tones. The woman couldn't talk gently if she tried!

Tapping at the door of Simon's room, Andrea opened it and peered into the office, and she was surprised to see Sir Humphrey seated at the desk Simon used when on duty.

'I beg your pardon, Sir Humphrey,' Andrea said instantly. 'I was hoping to find Mr Morrell here.'

'I'm sorry to be the one to disappoint you, Sister Chaston. But come in and wait for him, won't you? He's had an emergency on his hands, but the word is that he'll be through very shortly. I must say you look very pretty—if that's the right word—out of uniform. You're off duty, I take it.'

'Yes. There was just something I wanted to discuss with Mr Morrell.' Andrea entered the office and closed the door. Sir Humphrey had got to his feet at her entrance, and he pulled forward a chair for her, then sat down again when she was seated.

'I'm waiting to see him myself! I have some plans to talk over with him. We've got the go-ahead on the new wing, did you know?'

'Matron did say something about it last week.' Andrea nodded. 'We could certainly do with it.'

'Yes. Our present facilities are rather out of date, aren't they? But let's not talk shop while you're off duty. I understand that you've been doing very well here, Sister. When Sister Cole leaves I'm hoping to get you on my team.'

'Is Sister Cole thinking of leaving?' Andrea demanded, straightening in her seat.

'Perhaps I've said something I ought not to have passed on!' came the smooth reply. 'Could you forget that I said it?'

'Certainly, but you've made me very curious!' Andrea nodded slowly, and Sir Humphrey smiled.

'I'm sorry! You're only human, and curiosity is a dreadful blight, especially in a female. But I daren't say any more at this time, my dear.' He got to his feet, for once looking flustered. 'I think my chat with Simon can wait. He won't have his mind on me if you're here, anyway. Tell him I'll see him on Monday, would you?'

'I'll go if you would rather see him now, Sir Humphrey,' Andrea said quickly, getting to her feet. 'I'm sure your business with him is far more important than mine.'

'You gravely underrate yourself,' came the quick reply, and with a smile and a wave of his hand, the senior surgeon departed.

Andrea heaved a long sigh as she relaxed after his departure, and a frown touched her forehead. What had he meant about Sister Cole leaving? A pang touched Andrea's mind. Sister Cole had made her life a complete misery in the past, for some intangible reason best known to herself, and if she left the hospital it would be like getting a new lease on life! Andrea's pulses quickened at the thought and she moistened her lips. She felt as if a weight was being slowly removed from her shoulders.

But if Sister Cole left, whatever the reason, did it mean that Andrea herself would become Theatre Superintendent? The thought crossed her mind and she shook her head slowly. It was the height of her ambitions! But she dared not think of that eventuality. She had to keep level-headed! The situation was bad as it was, and it could only get worse if she permitted her mind to wander or not concentrate fully upon what was going on around her.

The crash of crockery falling upon a tiled floor aroused her from her thoughts and she glanced at the door which connected the office with the small kitchen that separated this room from her own office. It was a communal kitchen, used by herself and Sister Cole and the surgeons. Frowning, Andrea got to her feet and crossed to the door, opening it and peering into the kitchen.

Cora Bayliss was upon her knees in the kitchen, hastily gathering up the remains of the big china teapot. The door leading into Andrea's office stood open, and Andrea could see Sister Cole seated at her desk, staring into the kitchen with anger on her harshly set face. Cora looked up swiftly, and seemed confused. Her face was flushed and her eyes showed a mixture of excitement and shock.

'Oh!' The girl was obviously astonished at Andrea's appearance.

'I wondered what the crash was,' Andrea said. 'But there's a spare teapot in that top cupboard.'

'What are you doing here this morning, Sister?' Sister Cole's voice echoed across the kitchen. 'You're off duty! Can't you keep away from the place, or are you afraid that someone may take advantage of your absence?'

Andrea made no reply but stepped back into Simon's room and closed the door. She was trembling inside. Her heart was thudding powerfully and she felt a surge of dark emotion in her breast which threatened to stifle her. Why did Sister Cole have to be so nasty all the time?

She sat down beside Simon's desk again, and her thoughts remained upon Sister Cole. She tried to remember a time when her superior had not been sharp mannered, and she had to admit that of late Sister Cole's attitude had worsened, and was getting even worse. Then she heard footsteps in the corridor, and the next instant the door was opened and Simon appeared.

'Hello!' He was pleasantly surprised to see her, and Andrea got to her feet to greet him. He swept her into his arms for a moment, kissing her quickly before releasing her. 'This is a pleasant surprise. I was thinking about you as I came along the corridor. But there's nothing wrong, is there?'

'I just wanted to talk to you! Do you mind me dropping in on you like this?'

'Not at all! I'm happy to see you. But you do look worried about something.'

She told him about Sir Humphrey's presence in the office when she arrived, and Simon smiled.

'It will keep until Monday. He only wanted to go over some plans for the new wing. But what's on your mind, sweetheart?'

She told him about Peter Barlow, and saw his face stiffen. A shadow stared at her from his eyes, and then Simon shook his head.

'Poor chap! It's a distressing business! But it is all over for him now! I can understand you feeling quite upset, Andrea. He was a friend, wasn't he?'

'I knew him quite well! We went to school together!'

'And you're reproaching yourself now because you feel guilty that you didn't find the time to try and take him out of himself, is that it?'

'Something like it!' She sighed heavily. 'We both saw the state he was in when his mother died. I ought to have thought that being alone in that house would do something to him.'

'But you were too occupied with me, weren't you?' Simon regarded her thoughtfully. 'That's what is passing through your mind, isn't it? You're subconsciously blaming yourself for failing to prevent what happened to him.'

She nodded slowly. 'I feel that we have a duty towards our neighbours,' she said. 'We have to make the time to observe and help where we can.'

'I'm sure you do more than your share of caring for others,' he retorted. He glanced at his watch. 'Come on, I've finished for the morning. Let me drive you home!'

He called Switchboard and reported that he was leaving the hospital, and he gave Andrea's home telephone number as a reference in case he should be needed. They were at the door when the kitchen door opened and Cora Bayliss looked in.

'Would you like a cup of tea, Simon?' the girl demanded.

'No thank you. I'm leaving!' His tones were strictly unemotional, but Andrea could not help noticing the dead quality of his voice. He opened the door for Andrea and she walked out into the corridor. When she glanced back she saw Cora going back into the kitchen, her face expressionless but her eyes filled with an over-brightness. 'I have told her not to speak to me except in the line of duty,' Simon said as they walked along the corridor.

'I can understand your feelings after what happened before you came here, but don't you think you're being too hard on her?' Andrea asked softly.

He glanced at her quickly, and she heard his sharp intake of breath. 'You don't know her like I do,' he said slowly. 'If I gave her an inch it would be like admitting defeat. She's like that! I can't really describe her character, but nothing is too low for her to consider in the getting of her way. I found that out the hard way, Andrea, and even if I do seem rather harsh to you in the way I treat her, it is, I know, the only way to handle her.'

Andrea said no more! She could understand his attitude. He had lost a patient because of Cora Bayliss, and that was an unforgivable factor because Cora was a trained and skilled nurse. The patient always came first! That was the inflexible rule which applied to medicine in any of its branches! Cora had broken that rule and could never be forgiven.

On the way to her home, Andrea told Simon about the short conversation she'd had with Sir Humphrey, and when she repeated his words about Sister Cole leaving, Simon was struck with the same curiosity Andrea had felt.

'I haven't heard anything about Sister Cole leaving, have you?' he demanded.

'No. And I don't think she would leave willingly! This position is her whole life. But I can't help thinking over what Matron said. There have been a lot of complaints about Sister Cole recently, and she is being watched. I do hope they're not considering getting rid of her! That would be a tragedy.'

'They don't have grounds for dismissing her,' Simon said at once. 'She does her work very well, despite that unfortunate manner of hers. Sir Humphrey has asked me my opinion of her, but there was little I could tell him. I did say that she created a lot of tension in the department, where none was necessary, and that you were not to blame in any way for her attitude towards you.'

'There must be something wrong in her personal life, Simon. I have had the feeling for some time that she's being goaded by private worries.'

'Well you've been here longer than I have. What do you know about her?'

'That's the trouble! No one knows much about her! She lives alone in a flat, and if she ever goes out it's with Nurse Harmer.'

'And we know Nurse Harmer isn't very congenial company, don't we?' he demanded, shaking his head. 'Has she any family?'

'I don't think so. She was in an orphanage, so she hasn't any parents. I couldn't say about other relatives.'

'Perhaps that's half her trouble. Have you ever tried making friends with her?'

'I've bent over backwards trying to be friendly, but she snubs me cruelly. I'm worried about her, Simon. I wouldn't want to see her getting dismissed from her position here. I'm sure it would kill her.'

'Try and find something about her background. From what I have seen of her while I've been here I'm inclined to agree with you. She's got something worrying her. It may only be jealousy of you, but these things do get out of all proportion, as you know. Something ought to be done to help her. She's such a valuable nurse that it would be a pity to see her go down because of this unfortunate business of having her knife in you.' He glanced at her. They were nearing her home. 'You don't hate her for what she's doing to you, do you?'

'Of course not!' Andrea shook her head emphatically. 'I do feel sorry for her, especially as I think there's something wrong in her life. But every time I've tried to find out what it is she's snubbed me.'

'Nurse Harmer is her only friend, as you say. Why don't you have a word with her?'

'I will, tomorrow,' Andrea promised. 'This state of affairs can't go on, Simon. I'm sure Sister Cole is heading for a climax, and if she snaps inside, or does something wrong, it will be too late to try and help her then.'

'Good. I'm glad you're thinking like that. I'll back you all the way in anything you do. I agree with you. Sister Cole should be helped. And I think that while you're trying to help her you'll be helping yourself in this other matter. You're not really happy unless you are helping someone, are you?'

'It can be most unrewarding at times, but I like to do my bit to make the world go round just that little bit smoother.'

'I love you for your unselfishness, Andrea.' He slowed the car and turned into the driveway that led to her home. Let's spend the afternoon and evening together, shall we? I won't have to go back to the hospital unless there's an emergency. They can contact me here, or anywhere come to that. You look as if you need cheering up.'

'Reassuring,' she corrected. 'That's what I need. I have an uncanny feeling that everything is going to pieces. Perhaps it's because of what you told me about Cora. I am watching her like a hawk, but she seems so sweet on the surface. She's made friends with Sister Cole, and that takes some doing.'

'Unless Sister Cole realized that Cora would make a good ally against you.' Simon brought the car to a halt in front of the house. 'What's her manner been like towards you since Cora arrived?'

'Sharper!' Andrea shook her head. 'I did

think that they might get together against me, but there's no clear indication of it yet.'

'And knowing Cora, there won't be any warning if she's planning something against you. Don't be fooled by the calm, Andrea. Don't drop your guard at all.'

'I won't,' she said as they alighted from the car. 'I think I can see what kind of a woman Cora really is deep inside. It shows sometimes in her eyes and her face.'

'I know, I've seen it,' Simon retorted grimly.

They did spend the rest of Saturday together, and Andrea was reassured by Simon's company. But she knew reality lay always in the background, and after Simon had departed later that evening and she prepared to go to bed she knew that the next morning finally would dawn and she would be face to face with all the problems that seemed to be her lot . . .

On Sunday morning Andrea went to the hospital again, and she mentally crossed her fingers, knowing that Sister Cole would be on call and probably in the office working on the next week's duty lists and that Nurse Harmer should be around the Theatres. She heard nothing as she tiptoed past the office, and then she found Nurse Harmer in an anteroom.

Nurse Harmer eyed her suspiciously, more especially because Andrea was not in uniform. They hadn't spoken since Nurse Harmer had been transferred to Sister Cole's team, and

Andrea could tell by the girl's face that she regarded Andrea as the prime mover in her fall from grace.

'I must have a chat with you, Nurse,' Andrea said softly. 'I don't want Sister Cole to see me here, or learn why I'm talking to you.'

'What is it you want, Sister?' came the suspicious reply.

'I have to talk about Sister Cole. She's your friend, isn't she?'

'She is, but she's no friend of yours. What do you want to know about her?'

'Everything there is to know! It's surprising that I've known her for years and yet know practically nothing about her life.'

'What do you want to know about her? What's your reason?'

'Well you're her friend. Can't you see that she's not well? She's worried about something and it's getting worse.'

'She's not my friend, she's my aunt,' Nurse Harmer said softly.

'Your aunt!' Andrea was astonished.

'That's right, and I'm not telling you anything about her. I know you're not her friend. She's always had a lot of trouble from you, Sister. You're after her position here.'

'You should know me better than that! You've worked with me. You know I've never caused any trouble for Sister Cole. In fact you must recall that sometimes I've been in the wrong. But is that what she really thinks of

207

me? Is that what she's actually telling you about me?'

'What's that?'

'About me wanting to push her out so I can get her job!'

'That's what she thinks,' came the guarded reply.

'But I've never done anything to give her cause to believe that, Nurse. Can't you see that this bears out my suspicions? Your aunt needs help, and unless we can give it to her she may suffer a great deal.'

'There's a lot of truth in what she says. You were on the carpet with Matron last week, but nothing happened to you. Aunt Iris said then that they're keeping you to take charge of the new wing when it's built, and she'll be dismissed!'

'But that's ridiculous!' Andrea gasped, shaking her head in astonishment. 'Sister Cole is far more experienced than I! There'll be no question of her being passed over. The whole thing is preposterous, Nurse. Surely you can see that. Why do you think I've come to talk to you like this? I'm off duty, but I'm so concerned about Sister Cole that I've come in to see you.'

'Are you trying to say there's something wrong with my aunt? Is that the way you plan to get her out of her job? That's what Sister Bayliss said! You're too ambitious to be trusted. Ordinarily my aunt wouldn't be passed over, but if you can prove that she's not fit to do her duty properly then you would be her successor.' The girl shook her head vehemently. 'No, Sister. I'm not talking to you. I've got nothing to say. You had your knife in me, and you weren't satisfied until I was off your team. You don't have to try and pull the wool over my eyes. I know what you're up to, and I'll do everything I can to safeguard my aunt's rights.'

'If I can't convince you then I don't see what we can do to help Sister Cole,' Andrea said wearily. 'I can see it's no use talking to you. You don't want to know! But you'll realize too late that I am trying to help. Sister Bayliss would never help you, and any advice she gave you would be slanted towards helping her, I have no doubt. I never did anything against you, Nurse. You had to leave my team because Mr Morrell couldn't take any more of your inefficiency. You know you were not careful enough.'

'You're wasting your breath, Sister,' came the harsh reply. 'I think you'd better leave before my aunt does see you here. I've a good mind to tell her that you are trying to make mischief for her.'

Andrea sighed, and prepared to go on trying to make the girl see reason, but she could tell by Nurse Harmer's expression that she was wasting her time. She gave up then, and turned away, knowing that she was powerless to avert what she felt was a tragedy about to engulf them. All her instincts warned her to expect trouble, but she was helpless in the face of it, and she realized it as she left the department.

But she could not get away unnoticed. She was in the corridor leading past Sister Cole's office when the Sister herself appeared, and Andrea slowed her pace when she saw the woman. Sister Cole looked towards her, then took a closer look, and Andrea saw the change of expression which came to the woman's tense face.

'So you're here again! Are you living here now?' Sister Cole could not conceal her hatred, and her face was twisted with repressed passion that seemed to be slipping from her control. She waited until Andrea drew level with her, and there was violence showing in every line of her countenance. 'Are you still spying on me, Sister? What is it you're after? Is it just Mr Morrell? I know you're trying to take him away from Sister Bayliss! She's told me all about you! I knew my instincts couldn't be wrong. You are bad for this department, and Matron can't see it.'

'Sister, that's not true,' Andrea said sharply. She wondered if it would help to stand up against this woman instead of bending to her whims. But she didn't know what to do for the best.

'Don't trust her, Aunt!' Nurse Harmer came along the passage behind Andrea, and her voice was sharp and filled with malice. 'She was just asking me questions about you. I think she's going to try and prove that you're mentally ill, or under some kind of strain. I think that's the only way they can get rid of you. So don't believe her. Sister Bayliss would make a better Assistant for this department. You should try to do something about getting rid of her!'

Andrea firmed her lips. This looked like developing into a first class row, and that was to be avoided. But she reckoned without Sister Cole. The woman's face hardened at Nurse Harmer's words, and her dark eyes seemed to blaze with inner fury. Before Andrea realized what was happening her superior had stepped forward quickly, her strong hands lifting to seize hold of Andrea's long, chestnut hair. The next instant she was banging Andrea's head against the wall, and there was little Andrea could do about it.

Nurse Harmer came hurrying forward, and Andrea was barely aware that the girl tried to break her aunt's hold. A blackness seemed to swim before Andrea's gaze, and suddenly it swooped down to engulf her and she knew no more. There was just a nightmarish sense of falling into a deep, black, bottomless pit, then nothing . . .

CHAPTER THIRTEEN

Andrea's return to consciousness was heralded by a pain in her head which insisted upon arousing her. She opened her eyes and stared up at an unfamiliar tiled ceiling, and for a moment she tried to recollect her scattered thoughts. She fancied that she was in bed and that she ought to be thinking of getting up to go on duty. Then she realized that the tiled ceiling didn't belong to her bedroom, and suddenly it all came flashing back into her mind. Her thoughts picked up again to the moment she had blacked out, and she lifted her head quickly to look for Sister Cole. She found herself lying on the floor in the corridor, and Sister Cole was nowhere to be seen. But Nurse Harmer and Simon were coming fast along the corridor, and Andrea realized that the girl had gone for help.

'Andrea! Are you all right! What happened? I was coming into the Department as Nurse Harmer came running out, and she babbled something about Sister Cole trying to kill you!'

Andrea was only too aware of what Sister Cole had done to her. There was a large bump on the left side of her head, and her eyes were heavy with the pain that speared through her skull.

'I'm all right,' she said slowly, lifting her

hands and pressing her fingertips to her temples. 'But where is Sister Cole? I'm afraid she has lost control of herself.'

'She was here, still holding you when I ran to get help,' Nurse Harmer said frantically. 'I couldn't break her hold on you, Sister. I'm sorry. I didn't help matters when you came to talk to me, but I didn't believe you. I believed Sister Bayliss when she said you were trying to cause trouble. But I believe you now. My aunt was like a madwoman!'

'Your Aunt! Tell me what's going on here!' Simon, helping Andrea to her feet, glanced at the anxious face of Nurse Harmer.

'The details can wait until later,' Andrea said, moving her head experimentally. Simon was examining her, feeling for a fracture, and she saw relief in his dark eyes as he looked at her.

'I think you're all right,' he said. 'You've got a headache though, haven't you? Come along. You'd better sit down in the office and rest. I'll find Sister Cole and see what sort of state she's in.'

'I'll help you look for her,' Andrea said. 'I seem to be the cause of the trouble. I don't know why she should pick on me. I've never knowingly done her any injury.'

'That's beside the point. You've always been very close to her in the department, and that might have been the factor that brought her focus upon you.' Simon was looking anxiously

213

into Andrea's face and she made an effort to appear normal. She felt dazed, and apart from a headache she seemed to be all right. But she was concerned for her superior, and she started along the corridor to the office, hoping the Sister had taken refuge in there.

Nurse Harmer followed them, and Simon got ahead of Andrea when they reached the office. Andrea was tense and nervous. She fancied that Sister Cole had suffered a mental breakdown, and she feared the worst as Simon opened the office door. But the office was empty, and Simon's face was grim as he turned and looked at Andrea and Nurse Harmer.

'She didn't leave the department,' he said. 'We were at the entrance and she didn't go by me. She must still be here. We'd better look around for her. You stay with me, Andrea. If she sees you alone she may attack you again.'

Andrea had no intention of leaving Simon's side, and they went hurriedly to search the Theatres. They drew a blank, until they entered the new theatre to find Cora Bayliss busy there. The girl frowned when she saw Andrea at Simon's side, but she noted Andrea's dazed condition and guessed that something was wrong.

'Have you seen Sister Cole?' Simon demanded.

'Yes, she went through here a few moments ago, saying that she wanted some air. She went up to the roof!'

'Oh Lord!' Simon hurried towards the door at the far end. The new Theatre occupied the ground floor and there were offices and laboratories on the first floor. The flat roof had become something of an attraction to the nurses during their breaks and rest periods, and some of them had taken to using the roof for sunbathing.

Andrea felt a pang stab through her as she hurried after Simon, but he turned to her without breaking his stride.

'Stay away, Andrea. The sight of you might push her too far. I'll handle this, and you'd better come with me, Nurse Harmer. If she's your aunt then you might be able to exert some influence over her if she proves difficult in any way.'

Moving quickly, Simon departed and made for the stairs leading up to the roof. Andrea stayed where she was, and when she turned she found Cora Bayliss watching her closely.

'What happened?' the woman demanded.

Andrea explained hesitantly, and she saw Cora's expression tighten.

'I knew she was highly strung, and very upset,' Cora said. 'I thought you were the cause of her trouble.'

'She picked on me for some unknown reason,' Andrea retorted. 'But you got closer to her in the past week than I've managed to do in several years. Did she have anything to say that might have indicated to you the causes for her behaviour?'

'She was jealous of you. That much was obvious. She was afraid you would take over her job. She felt you had your knife into Nurse Harmer!'

'Who turns out to be her niece!' Andrea shook her head slowly. 'I've never done anything to give Sister Cole the idea that I might have been ambitious enough to want her position in the department.'

'I've revised my own opinion of you in the week that I've been here,' Cora said. 'I was ready to fight you tooth and nail for Simon, but it soon became apparent to me that I would never succeed. This may not be the time or the place to tell you, but I've given up any idea I had of trying to get him back. What happened before we came here was too much for his sensitive nature. I can see that now. I was a fool to come here. But I never stop to think about my actions.'

Andrea felt a pang of relief inside, but she knew better than to take the woman's word. She glanced anxiously towards the door through which Simon had departed, and she wished he would appear. He ought to have checked the roof by now. She began to move towards the door despite his orders to stay away. If they were having trouble with Sister Cole then they might need help. She glanced at Cora.

'Come along,' she ordered. 'We'd better see

216

if there's anything we can do to help. They must have found Sister Cole by now.'

Cora's face was white as she went with Andrea, and they ascended the stairs, passing the first floor and continuing up to the roof. They passed through an iron door at the very top of the stairs and walked out on to the roof. The sunlight was brilliant after the dim interior of the theatres, and Andrea narrowed her eyes as she looked around.

The flat roof was surrounded at its perimeter by iron railings set in concrete, and Nurse Harmer was standing by the railings at the far end of the roof. Andrea paused and looked around for Simon, and she was horrorstruck when she saw his head and shoulders showing above the roof level. He was grasping a rail and hanging on for dear life.

Cora uttered a gasp of shock, but it was Andrea who moved first. She ran across the roof and paused at Nurse Harmer's side. She looked over the edge of the roof and saw that Sister Cole was standing on the iron fire escape, on the outside of the railings, and Simon had hold of the woman by the hand and was hanging on for dear life to prevent her throwing herself to the ground two storeys below.

Simon was talking earnestly to Sister Cole, but as Andrea arrived he was trying to get Sister Harmer to join him in holding Sister

Cole.

'I daren't!' the girl replied in gasping tones. 'I'm afraid of heights. I'll fall if I come over there.' She was gripping the rail where she stood with clutching fear.

'Then go and get help!' Simon's tones betrayed his great tension. 'I can't hold on to her much longer.'

'I'm here, Simon,' Andrea said quickly, and he turned his head to look up at her, relief showing on his sweating face. 'What can I do?'

'Can you get over here on to the fire escape and seize hold of Sister Cole? I need to get a fresh grip on her, but she's not holding on, and if I let go of her she'll fall to the ground.'

Andrea did not hesitate. She slipped between the railings and stepped on to the platform at the top of the fire escape, trying desperately not to look down at the ground floor below. She had to put one foot on the top rung of the iron ladder and brace herself against the railings, ducking under Simon's outstretched arm, and she noticed that he had interlaced his fingers with Sister Cole.

As Andrea put her arms around Sister Cole's thin waist she was struck by the woman's impassiveness. Sister Cole didn't seem to be aware of her surroundings and she did not struggle. She was a dead weight in Andrea's arms, and when Simon let go of the Sister's hand in order to take a fresh grip, the weight almost dragged Andrea off balance, and for one awful moment she felt that she and Sister Cole would go plunging to the ground. But she braced her thighs against the low rail that was between them and hung on grimly.

Simon was coming down on to the platform. Andrea looked up and saw Nurse Harmer still standing petrified by the top railings, and Cora Bayliss appeared at the girl's side. She seemed in little better state, and there was panic in her pale eyes as she stared down at Andrea.

The next moment Simon was at Andrea's side, and he put his arms around Sister Cole.

'Let's try and lift her back on to the platform,' he said in thick tones.

Andrea exerted her strength, but Sister Cole was heavy, and as she felt herself being moved, the woman seized hold of the railings and clung desperately. Simon looked up. Andrea, looking into his face, saw anger and concern mingled in his taut expression.

'For the Lord's sake, do something,' he gasped. 'Cora, get help. Get the porters up here. Anyone to help. Don't stand there like an idiot! Get moving.'

Cora nodded, jerked out of her shock by his harsh voice, and she turned and hurried away. But Nurse Harmer was beyond helping, and she clung to the railings and stared down at them, her eyes blank and filled with shock.

'Sister!' Simon was trying to get through to Sister Cole. 'I want you to climb over the rails.

We've got you. Don't be afraid. You're not going to fall.'

Sister Cole muttered some unintelligible reply, and let go her hold on the top rail. She swayed outwards, and despite Andrea's desperate effort to hang on to her, the weight of her body broke Andrea's grip. She almost slipped off the platform herself, and grabbed desperately at the rail with one hand while her other hand tried to find fresh grip on the woman.

Simon's face was a matter of inches from Andrea's, and she looked into his eyes and saw the worry in their dark depths.

'Hang on to her, Andrea,' he pleaded. 'But be careful. Don't fall, for Heaven's sake.'

'We'd better not move her. Let's try to hold her until help comes,' Andrea said, and he nodded, his head pressed against Sister Cole's shoulder.

'She was standing up on the roof, leaning on the rails when I saw her,' Simon said in panting tones. 'But when I approached her she started to climb over the rails. I was so surprised that she almost got clean over before I could move. Then I grabbed her and she jumped. I happened to catch her hand, but she would have gone if she hadn't been standing directly over the fire escape. Her feet landed on the top rail, and I managed to hold on to her while I got over the rail into the position you found me in. But she slipped down outside the platform, and I was almost losing my hold on her when you came up. Nurse Harmer was too petrified to do anything to help.'

Andrea nodded, hanging on grimly to Sister Cole. The iron rail was boring into her hip, hurting sharply, but she dared not move. Simon tried talking to Sister Cole again, but the woman paid no heed. She seemed to be in a strange kind of conscious coma.

'Sister, can you hear me?' Simon said again. 'It's all right. You're quite safe. You've been taken ill and I want to help you. This is Simon Morrell! Can you hear me?'

There was no sign of recognition in Sister Cole, and Andrea looked up into the woman's hard face, remembering all the times they had clashed over insignificant matters, and she knew now that she had been correct in thinking that Sister Cole had been mentally ill. Perhaps strain had overcome her! But it had been overpowering her for a long time.

'They're taking my department away from me!' Sister Cole spoke suddenly, and surprisingly clearly. 'I've got to leave! They're kicking me out and putting Sister Chaston in charge. I always knew she was after my job.'

'You're mistaken, Sister,' Simon said, frowning as Andrea looked at him. 'You're too valuable to be dismissed, and they have no reason to get rid of you! As for Sister Chaston, she wouldn't take your job under those circumstances. I was talking to her recently and she said she was worried about you. She has only your good interests at heart. Now why don't you climb back over that rail and we'll get you safely into bed? You need a good long rest.'

'Sister Bayliss told me she overhead Sir Humphrey telling Sister Chaston that when I left the department he wanted Sister Chaston to work with him!' Sister Cole spoke emphatically, her words formed slowly and with hatred. 'After all the years I've worked at this hospital. I've always put my duty first. Now they're going to kick me out. Let go of me! I want to die. I can't go on any longer.'

She began to struggle, and Andrea gritted her teeth and clung desperately to her superior. Her thoughts were remotely flitting through her mind, and she recalled that Sir Humphrey had said something about Sister Cole leaving. Cora Bayliss had been in the kitchen at that time, and she must have been eavesdropping! Horror filled Andrea as once again she almost pitched over the rails, but Simon was well set and he had both arms around Sister Cole. Between them they managed to calm her again, and then Simon began talking softly.

'You should never listen to anything that is repeated from hearsay, Sister,' he said. 'I don't know what Sir Humphrey actually said to Sister Chaston, but I do know that they want to put her in charge of the new wing and the department when it is built and in operation. But you're not going to be pushed out or dismissed. I don't know where you got that idea from. Matron is due to retire about the time the new wing will be ready, and it's been arranged that the assistant matron will take over. That leaves a vacancy for an assistant matron, and the position is going to be offered to you.'

Andrea listened with surprise in her mind, but she was pleased by the revelation, and she sensed that Simon was telling the truth and not just trying to humour Sister Cole. But the woman was struggling again, and Andrea lost her footing on the edge of the platform and slipped down the iron ladder that led down to the lower platform. She lost her hold completely on Sister Cole, and flung her arms wide to stop her own fall. She caught hold of a rung on the ladder and her fingers closed convulsively about it, arresting her plunge. She thought her right arm would be torn out of its sockets, but she quickly secured a hold with her left hand, hung suspended for a moment, fighting the weakness that filled her, and then she started back to the platform again, where Simon was struggling desperately with Sister Cole.

'Are you all right?' Simon gasped, and Andrea nodded, quite unable to speak for a moment. 'Take her under the chin and exert some pressure on her head.' Simon seemed almost at the end of his strength. 'We've got to get her on to the platform.'

There was little space in which to work, and Andrea fought down her fear of heights and tried to prevent the trembling that gripped her from overwhelming her. She reached out and placed a hand under Sister Cole's chin. The woman had her back to them now, and was trying to lean forward in order to plummet to the ground. Bracing herself, Andrea pulled back hard, and as Sister Cole's head came back her weight readjusted. Simon pulled at the same time, and the next instant Sister Cole came crashing back over the top rail to fall heavily upon them. She struggled fervently to break their hold but they clung desperately to her and held her.

A few moments later there was movement on the roof above them. Two porters had arrived, and as soon as they sized up the situation they descended to the platform and helped overpower Sister Cole. After a brief struggle, the woman was secured and carried bodily up to the roof, then borne away into a side ward.

Simon helped Andrea on to the roof from the fire escape, and Andrea was near to collapse. Her head ached intolerably and her right arm felt as if it had been dragged from its socket. She leaned against Simon, who put his arms about her, and Sister Bayliss stood watching them. Simon was breathing heavily from his exertions with Sister Cole. His face was pale and his hands trembled as they held Andrea.

'You added the last straw to the situation, Cora,' he said sharply. 'You told Sister Cole what you overheard yesterday morning in my office between Sir Humphrey and Andrea. But you didn't hear the half of it. You didn't care! You were only interested in getting some advantage from it. You saw the friction that existed between Sister Cole and Andrea, and you were up to your old tricks in trying to get it to work for you. I doubt if you'll ever learn your lesson, but I suggest you start looking for a position at another hospital and get out of our lives before I lose my reason and do something to you that I may regret for the rest of my life.'

Andrea looked up quickly into his face, but said nothing, and she saw Cora Bayliss smile thinly.

'Don't worry. I decided this morning when things started going wrong that I would leave here. I know I made a mistake coming. So I'll be on my way again as soon as I can make it.' Cora turned away and departed, and Simon sighed heavily in relief.

'What about Sister Cole?' Andrea demanded.

'We can look after her now,' he said. 'But what about you, Andrea? I thought I'd lost you a couple of times on that platform. You look badly shaken. You'd better let me drive you home, and if you rest up today you shouldn't have any ill effects from this.'

'I can't go home. Sister Cole was on duty, and as she's ill then I'll have to take over.' Andrea's voice was strong as she spoke. Duty always came first, and the knowledge that she would have to stand by made her feel stronger immediately.

Simon took a deep breath and held it for a moment. He looked down into her eyes. They were alone on the roof now, and the brightness of the morning bathed them with warmth.

'I have the feeling that all our troubles are over,' he said gently, and kissed her.

Andrea relaxed against him. For a moment she thought she would lose her senses as reaction to her shock struck through her. But there was a stronger emotion alive in her mind and his kiss seemed to release it. She clung to him, her face burning at their contact, and his arms were strong about her slim body. He kissed her until she gasped for breath, and then he released her slowly.

'Let's go and get a cup of coffee,' he said gently. 'You were magnificent on that platform, Andrea. You were scared half to death, I could see, but it was duty calling, and you saw it through like the dedicated nurse you are.'

She suppressed a shudder, and knew that some of her dreams in the future would transport her back to those terrible moments when Sister Cole's life was in the balance. But there were other dreams to compensate for the bad ones, and some of those good dreams seemed about to materialise. She knew all her ambitions would be realized, but now she wanted nothing more than to be loved by Simon.

His lips very gently touched her quivering mouth, and their contact filled her with ecstasy.

'I love you, Simon!' She spoke so softly that she fancied he did not hear her. But he tightened his grasp upon her and she knew he had heard.

'I love you with all my heart, Andrea,' he replied.

They kissed again, and now words were quite unnecessary. The sun was hot upon them as they stood in its stark light, and Andrea closed her eyes against its brilliance. Tension fled from them and their choking shock began to recede before the onset of finer emotions and hopes. They both knew instinctively that everything in future would be all right, and all they asked for was an even chance to prove it. The fact that they were very much in love provided a better than even opportunity.

Then an apologetic voice spoke behind them, and they drew apart to find Nurse Harmer standing in the doorway leading down into the hospital.

'I'm sorry to disturb you,' the girl said. 'But there's an emergency case of appendicitis coming in. Can we be in Theatre as soon as possible?'

'We're coming, Nurse,' Simon said gently, and Andrea smiled.

Duty called! It was always so! She took a deep breath and held it for a moment, then released it in a long, shuddering sigh.

'All right?' Simon demanded as Nurse Harmer hurried away.

'Very much so,' she replied, and she was completely happy for the first time in her life!

We hope you have enjoyed this Large Print book. Other Chivers Press or G.K. Hall & Co. Large Print books are available at your library or directly from the publishers.

For more information about current and forthcoming titles, please call or write, without obligation, to:

Chivers Press Limited
Windsor Bridge Road
Bath BA2 3AX
England
Tel. (01225) 335336

OR

G.K. Hall & Co.
P.O. Box 159
Thorndike, Maine 04986
USA
Tel. (800) 223-2336

All our Large Print titles are designed for easy reading, and all our books are made to last.